PENGUIN BOOKS

MANNING CLARK: COLLECTED SHORT STORIES

Manning Clark was born in Sydney in 1915, and educated at Melbourne Grammar School, the University of Melbourne and Balliol College, Oxford. A teacher and university lecturer, in 1946 he decided to concentrate on the teaching and writing of Australian history. Among his publications are *A History of Australia* in five volumes, *A Short History of Australia, Select Documents in Australian History, Occasional Writings and Speeches, In Search of Henry Lawson,* and *Meeting Soviet Man.* Emeritus Professor of History at the Australian National University, Manning Clark is married and the father of six children.

MANNING CLARK:

COLLECTED SHORT STORIES

PENGUIN BOOKS

Penguin Books Australia Ltd,
487 Maroondah Highway, P.O. Box 257
Ringwood, Victoria, 3134, Australia
Penguin Books Ltd,
Harmondsworth, Middlesex, England
Penguin Books,
40 West 23rd Street, New York, N.Y. 10010, U.S.A.
Penguin Books (Canada) Limited,
2801 John Street, Markham, Ontario, Canada L3R 1B4
Penguin Books (N.Z.) Ltd,
182-190 Wairau Road, Auckland 10, New Zealand

The first twelve stories published 1969 by Angus & Robertson Publishers as *Disquiet and other stories*
Published in Penguin, 1986

Copyright © Manning Clark, 1986

Offset from the Angus & Robertson edition with new setting by Leader Composition
Made and printed in Australia by The Dominion Press–Hedges & Bell

Clark, Manning, 1915–
Collected short stories.

New ed.
ISBN 0 14 009294 3 (pbk.).

I. Title. II. Title : Disquiet and other stories.

A823'.3

For Andrew, Rowland, and Benedict

ACKNOWLEDGEMENTS

Most of these stories appeared first in periodicals. The author is grateful to the editors of the *Bulletin, Quadrant, Partisan, Prometheus, Melbourne University Magazine* and *Australian Short Stories* for permission to republish them in a revised form.

M.C.

CONTENTS

Disquiet

IN THE Phillip Island Hotel at Cowes just four years after
the end of the war to end all wars, a group of locals had
gathered for a "spot" and a yarn about old times. One man
drank alone. He was old Tug, the local night-soil man. He
seemed past caring. They, at least, had spruced themselves up
for the occasion; they had had a dip in a hot tub, had rubbed
themselves clean, and plastered oil on their hair, and put on
suits. But Tug, the low bastard, had turned up as usual dressed
in a filthy woollen shirt, and filthy dungarees held up by a
piece of rope tied round his huge protruding belly. He sat on
a stool in the corner of the bar, a toothless slobberer, who had
guzzled so much beer that he had lost the power of speech, and
could only manage swinish grunts, but still managed to get the
barman to understand his needs by pointing at the empty glass.

Then when his money ran out, and the barman refused to
put ticks against his name on that slate kept under the bar for
any man who was having an attack of the "shorts" without any
corresponding weakening of his thirst, old Tug muttered some

obscenity, climbed down off his stool, and staggered towards the others and asked, finding the words to meet his very pressing need — "Which of yous buggers is going to buy an old digger a drink?"

The three of them said nothing. It happened every Saturday night — Tug cadging money for his knock-out drop, swaying as he surveyed them from head to foot, followed by his drunken attempt to say the wounding thing, to rouse their guilt as well as their shame before he walked out into the night, only managing some short question such as "Anyhow, who'd want to drink with you three shits?" for Tug's complaint against humanity for despitefully using him never went beyond his dismay that no one would buy him a drink.

The other three remained to enjoy the relief of his going. One of the few times Harry Rourke was ever seen to smile was when Tug finally staggered out of the bar at the Phillip Island Hotel every Saturday night. Soon after Harry had come back from the war he had heard that his wife was known as the local morgue, and, when he had asked, guileless as ever, why one so warm and friendly as his wife, Queenie, should be likened to the place of the dead, he had been told — not brutally, not to wound, because Harry was known as the whitest man on the island — but because the locals had their own code of behaviour. One of the prohibitions was for their wives — "Thou shalt not monkey round." So the locals arranged for his cobber, Charlie East, to tell him — not eye to eye but staring at the floor, the words coming slowly, saying he didn't want to do this to anyone, but a man ought to know a morgue was the place where all the local stiffs went. And Harry Rourke had gone so silent that the locals said you could not get a word out of the man even edgeways. When he went out he turned up the lapels on his coat so that the world could not peer in. The locals whispered that if he did not shake a leg, he would lose his farm as well as his wife, because as his other cobber, Billy Gossop used to say, moping around never put no splondoolicks in any man's till.

If it had not been for his two cobbers, Billy Gossop and Charlie East, and the sessions they had together every Saturday night at the Phillip Island Hotel, Harry might have done what he sometimes threatened to do. He might have ended it all. Of course, they told him not to be so bloody silly, and he told them with unwonted spirit that he was not being bloody silly, and put it, "Nobody knows what I've been through." Billy Gossop used to tell him that in his opinion a man who felt sore with life ought to put a glass of beer to his lips rather than a razor to his throat, and not to be such a bloody mug as to join the long-term men in the local bone-yard, and how the brass rail round the bar was the only communion rail a man ever knew, and, anyhow, what else had he bloody well expected out of life?

For Billy had his own source of pain. As the evening wore on, he would stand with his back to the wall, legs bent a shade, and wide open, using the palms of his hands like a priest turning to the faithful, drawing them, as it were, to that great mother, the Church, just as Billy wanted to draw men unto him — but knew he could not, or should not, or perhaps that it was better not to. So he made instead this limited gesture, his own "Come unto me", knowing that it would end with his backside beginning to slide down the wall and some feverish puffs at his cigarette, like a young girl wondering whether she could finish her first cigarette before being sick; but with a great smile, the smile of a man who felt tenderly towards everyone, but had never been allowed, or, rather, never dared to show it, until Harry Rourke put his arms round him and smiled, too, and said "It's time for me to get you home, Billy boy."

Charlie East, Harry's other great cobber, was a chicory farmer who did some cray-fishing to get a crust for his wife and his kids. He was said to be the only man who had pulled crays off the wall of the blowhole at the Nobbies on north wind days, when that great green swell lay still, and ceased to roar and hiss and foam. He was a huge man, Charlie, big boned, with a white moustache, lips tanned by beer and tobacco, with face and gestures to mark him out from the crowd, but stooped by years over the cray-pot and the chicory row, earning that crust for his family on an island where the soil, as Billy Gossop used to say, was as sour as life, and that was saying something.

From time to time Charlie would lean forward, and stroke the underside of his moustache, as though if nature, or the fates, had been kinder he might have attracted attention in high

3

places, but was destined instead to hoe his fields in the autumn, winter and spring, and set his cray-pots in the summer, and brood over or try to find someone who would understand his own source of shame. So that every Saturday night when Harry Rourke announced it was time to get Billy Gossop home, Charlie would insist that Billy was good for at least one more, and turn to Harry as though, maybe, here in the bar room, there must be someone who would understand, someone to wash away the guilty stains, and say, "I tell you, my brother and I decided to toss a coin. We tossed a coin — I had no idea what was going to happen to him. Do you think I would have agreed to toss a coin if I had thought he was going to be killed? We could not both go. They wouldn't let us. So, as I told you, we tossed a coin . . . we tossed a bloody coin, I tell you, a bloody coin."

Then Harry Rourke said, "I know, Charlie", and Billy Gossop squeezed his arm quite tenderly and told him not to be so bloody mad with himself, that everyone knew his brother was one of the whitest men who had ever lived, and everyone with any decency knew that he, Charlie, was every bit as much a white man as his brother — and how Charlie ought to listen to his own cobbers, and take no notice of that runt, Val O'Donoghoe. The man was an animal.

Then the three of them walked together, swaying slightly past that simple column of good Woolomai rock on which was cut in letters of gold the names of those who had volunteered to fight for King and Country. Charlie read slowly the names of W. Gossop and H. Rourke and then the name of one who had paid the supreme sacrifice — E. East — and paused, and swayed, and said, "Jesus Christ".

As those three swaying figures stood there before the column, three human silhouettes, fumbling for the words or the gestures with which to comfort and relieve each other, old Tug was having trouble with his horse. It had stopped in the sand patch on the Rhyll road, and refused to move. When old Tug took the whip and stood up in the dray, and brought the whip down hard on the horse's eyes, saying drunkenly, "I'll teach you who's master here", the horse reared, tilting the dray; Tug fell out of the back and rolled under the rear left wheel, and

the horse and dray lurched backwards and killed old Tug —
though not before he called out, "You'll pay for this, you
bastard."

On the Monday morning, when he heard what had
happened, Billy Gossop decided, as he put it, that seeing how
they had treated the old bugger while he was alive, and since
he was after all an old digger, the least they could do was to
give him a decent funeral. So he decided to go the rounds of
the local parsons. He started with the Presbyterian minister
because as the man seemed to be so awfully fond of talking
about sinners, it might be a kindness to ask him to bury one.
He was a bit surprised when the parson told him he was not
going to make a mockery of that promise of glorious resurrection by reciting the words over the dead body of a notorious
drunkard, whom God, in his infinite mercy, would send to
perdition. So Billy went off to San Remo to see the Catholic
priest, who was said to be very accommodating to the locals who
went to see him about their lapses with women. Judging by the
way those O'Donoghoes went on, you would think he'd been
giving them some good tips. One of them had told him a man
felt cleaner after being in the box with the Father than after
the weekly bath. But the priest said simply he could not look
at it — "He was not one of ours. But why don't you approach
the Anglican parson in Cowes, Mr Gossop? There's a man who,
on his own confession, Mr Gossop, wants to be remembered
as the man who was all things to all men. Try him."

When Billy put the question to the new Anglican vicar of
Phillip Island, the Reverend Thomas Hogan, T.H.L. of Moore
College, Sydney, and an old digger, the latter wanted to say
as the Catholic priest had said, "I couldn't look at it", but was
held back by the thought that if Billy should press for reasons,
he would either have to plead some lame-duck excuse such as
being too busy when everyone on the island used to say a man
must have a hell of a lot of time to himself every week if he only
has to preach and pray for a crust, or he might let it slip that
there would be a poor plate at evensong on Sunday if the ladies
in the congregation heard he had buried a toss-pot like old
Tug. But how could he let on to Billy Gossop, a butcher's
assistant, that the collection, the free-will offering, the oppor-

tunity to let their light so shine before God that they may see His good works and glorify their Father, was all that he ever thought of. So there was a silence between them during which the Reverend Hogan's mind moved right away from worldly considerations.

Would not the burial of old Tug provide a glorious opportunity for him to teach the locals that a man should accept the whole of God's creation, the hideous, the hateful, the loathsome as well as the beautiful, the weak as well as the strong, the tortoises as well as the hares, toothless slobberers like old Tug as well as the comely? Why this should be so was a mystery — God's mystery. Now, we saw through a glass darkly, but a day would come when we would see it all face to face. He was as sure of that as he was that he was standing there in front of Billy Gossop. Had not his Saviour predicted that the last would be first? Had not his Saviour let drop the even stronger remark that on the resurrection morning, when, as the hymn reminds us, soul and body meet once more, there would be no giving in marriage? Was it not possible that on that day when old Tug put off his corruptible body and took on incorruption, he might stand before them in the body of Apollo? The longer he lived the more convinced he was that there was a great mystery at the heart of things.

Not that he could tell Billy *that*, let alone tell it to his wife who would be sure to say she wished he would not go on that way because it made her feel he must be very peculiar. The plain fact was that he could not tell it to anyone at all, because whenever he had tried to tell people what he believed the men had laughed and said, "Our ickle man's quite a poet", and the women had either looked at him as though he were peculiar or said tartly, "How very unhealthy", and forsaken him.

So all he could manage, or risk were some sentimental words which hinted at the great storm raging inside him.

"My dear old mother," he told Billy, "taught me that it takes all sorts to make a world."

Then he shook him so warmly by the hand, at the same time gripping his forearm so tightly with the left hand that, as Billy put it later to his cobbers at the Phillip Island Hotel, "I thought for a moment he was going to put the hard word on me — no, fair dinkum, I did. But when he began to look so vacant like, he made me feel so queer that I crept away."

The Reverend Mr Hogan looked as though he was up in the clouds, because life on earth had suddenly presented a problem to which he did not know the answer. The problem was how to tell his wife what he had decided to do. If he told her that he had promised to bury old Tug, she would be certain to say she wished he would not spend his time with the "lowest of the low". To which, if he was trapped into reminding her of Christ's saying that the last shall be first, she might be tempted to reply that that would not be much to his liking, as he had spent all his talents on being first in this world. And, if he were not to tell her and she found out, as she was bound to do, because you couldn't keep anything from them, then she would start crying again at night in bed, and when he asked her to tell him for God's sake what was the matter, she would tell him she had hoped he would never lie to her again . . . and he did not know whether he could stand that again. The fact was he would be punished if he talked, and if he didn't then he would be punished for not talking and told, "I know you can't talk to me about the things that touch you deeply."

So while Billy Gossop was staring at him and wondering why that face of warmth and animation had become cold and immobile, the Reverend Hogan was deciding that he would take his boy with him, the young Charles Hogan — the one comfort left from a union which he had entered in the hope that the two of them, man and wife, would become one flesh, only to find the wonder of a man with a maid change into a battlefield in which he was taught some painful lessons about his own swinishness.

Sure enough, when he told her that night, staring into the fire, and not risking to look at her eye to eye, for both knew too well that only led on, not to a tooth for a tooth, but certainly to a blemish for a blemish, she had said, stabbing her needle back into the pincushion, and tapping its head hard with the thimble, "Why do you want Charles to mix with the lowest of the low?"

He thought of reminding her of what their blessed Lord, when He had dwelt amongst them, had said about those who did it unto the least of the little ones, and how He had lived His earthly life, not with the Philistines or the Pharisees and the upright ones, those ones who did not need to stop·because they had not started, but with the publicans, like the manager of the Phillip Island Hotel, and Magdalenes, like Queenie Rourke. Only he knew all too well she would say that if he was so fascinated by queer people he ought to live with them, only he must not expect her to go with him, and he would say angrily, "God spare my days, woman. What do you think the women on the island would say if they knew the wife of the vicar had branded them as God's whores?"

And perhaps there would be a scene — shoutings — more angry words from which he could only extricate himself by asking her to forgive him and she would say again, "There's nothing to forgive." Anything, he thought, rather than that Hell again. So he kept quiet.

As he harnessed old Ginger to the jinker the following afternoon for the drive to the cemetery, there was none of that banter and boasting, none of that "I tell you, boy, there's nothing a horse enjoys more than having her mane combed by a man with a cricketer's flick of the wrist and a pianist's fingers, except for a tickle in the right place, if you see what I mean, boy." And old Ginger would whinny, and he would smack her on the rump with the flat of his hand, and say to the boy, "It's her way, boy, of showing she's pleased to see us," and father and boy would look gently at each other and a smile would spread all over the father's face.

But on that afternoon the vicar's face was calm, flat as the sea before a great storm breaks. For the man had in his heart that hell of a man who has shown his view to a woman, who has responded with a condemnation of his whole life. So instead of receiving the benefits of the cricketer's wrist and the pianist's fingers, old Ginger felt those jabs of a man who was angry with his brother — a pain which caused her to make angry moves to get the bit out of her mouth. And when the vicar told the boy to lower the shafts of the jinker and hold them steady — "Now I said steady, boy, none of that shaft stuttering from you today, or I'll tear the hide off you" — old Ginger suddenly stamped and reared up on her hind legs, from where she looked down on the boy with such terror and menace in her eyes that the boy dropped the shafts he was holding and the vicar turned on him and shouted, "God spare my days, boy, you'd fall over on a billiard table. I should have asked your brother to help me harness the horse."

The boy, sensing it was to be a day of shouting and abuse followed by flattery and affection, began to wonder what possible excuse he could give for not going, without provoking his father to worse rages. And then the vicar kneed old Ginger hard in the belly, and said, "After I give her another one with the knee, she'll breathe, boy. Now the minute she breathes — are you listening to me, boy? — tighten the girth. You're quicker at it than your brother, boy. Ready . . . that's it, well done, boy, well done. By God, boy, you're as quick as greased lightning. I tell you, boy, we'll be off in two jiffys from now."

And so they were. As they swung out on to the back-beach road, the vicar rose from his seat and lashed old Ginger on the rump, and called, "Gee-up, gee-up. We're late enough as it is. You know, boy, they can say what they like about me, but I'm a beggar for being on time. And I'll tell you another thing, boy, you won't catch me with one wheel of the jinker on the crown of the road, and the other on the side of the road. That's the mistake old Bilson makes. A great man, boy, old Bilson, to turn a jinker arse-a-peak."

And he looked at the boy, not so much for applause — because unlike old Bilson and all the other old fogeys on the island he could stop a jinker turning "arse-a-peak" — but because in life he had learned how to steer his way between the stones that could bring a man to his destruction.

As man and boy swayed gently to the rhythm of the trot, and the thud of hoof on black soil assumed the regularity of a musical figure, the father asked, "Do you hear it, boy? What's it remind you of? Listen, boy . . . dumpity-dumpity-dump. Now, don't tell me, boy, you don't recognize it . . . a clever customer like you? It's the same as dickory, dickory, dock. . . . Listen, boy, don't tell me you can't hear it."

So the boy thought he would risk asking his father a question to which he badly wanted to know the answer — "What's going to happen to old Tug, dad?"

The father wanted to answer just as the Saviour of men had answered the simple fishermen of Galilee when they put their questions to Him. He wanted to bring all manner of men unto him by saying the memorable thing, but instead found himself, as ever, led into talking about himself.

"You are becoming a thoughtful customer, boy. . . . When you get older, boy, you must read Watch Ditchfield on *Who Moved the Stone?* Watch Ditchfield's the man for Christian apologetics — that's defending the truths of Christianity, boy. I know what's on your mind, boy. You want to know what is going to happen to Tug. That's a good question, boy, a very good question. Our Saviour didn't say much about what was going to happen in the Resurrection morning — except that there was to be no giving in marriage, if you see what I mean, boy. Tug does not need his old body any more; he's going to get a new body; God's going to give him one; he's like a man whose clothes have worn out, God can do anything, boy, he can move mountains, heal the sick, make the last first — it's going to be easy for God to make a new body for old Tug."

"Then, dad, why doesn't God make new bodies for all of us . . . and new clothes for Queenie Rourke, and all the women on the island?"

"He will, in time, boy, you mark my words — only not in this world, boy, there's tribulation and sorrow in this world . . . God's keeping his clothes for a time when true joys are to be found."

He wanted to tell the boy he believed a day would come when all mankind would be clothed in heavenly raiment and the earth would be full of the glory of the Lord. God, he believed, would forgive everyone — a day would come when everyone would be whiter than snow, but, as the boy had never seen snow, he thought perhaps he had better keep off that. That was the difficulty. That was why he was tempted to believe that gloomy remark in Ecclesiastes, "There is one alone, and there is not a second." The words reminded him of a dream he had had recently about his dead father, in which he had walked down to the jetty at Cowes, and seen his father preparing his fishing lines in a rowing boat tied to the jetty. And he had seen clearly, as one does in dreams, that his father knew, not just how to handle fishing lines, but something more — some big thing about life; but when he had asked him to show him how to row that boat, his father had not even lifted his eyes off the hooks and sinkers, let alone stretched out his arms to him . . . and he had woken up wondering whether perhaps life, too, was like that, that those who knew the way either could not or would not tell it to anyone else, not even to those most in need of the helping hand — that, as the preacher says in Ecclesiastes, "There is one alone, and there is not a second."

In an hour's time he would stand beside the coffin of a monstrously ugly man over whose remains he would recite those beautiful words about departing this life in the hope of a glorious resurrection from the dead, when everyone knew the only hope old Tug ever entertained was that someone would buy him another beer. It was always the same — filth was beauty's neighbour. Perhaps that was why the Saviour had made that point about the tares and the wheat. He could see that himself. Why then could he not explain it to the boy sitting beside him? Why was it that he could detect a pattern of sound as old Ginger's hooves thudded on the black soil: he knew it was dumpity, dumpity, dump, but all he could think of was dickory, dickory, dock. Inwardly he soared, but what came out was banal, trivial and common.

As the jinker carrying the father and the boy moved into the sand patch at the foot of the cemetery hill, and the horse dropped into a walk, Billy Gossop, Charlie East and Harry Rourke were just about to leave the bar at the Phillip Island Hotel where they had paused for longer than they had planned because the first time they had made a move to go, Billy had reminded them that as it would be an awfully long time before they breasted the communion rail again, they had better make sure they had "enough on board". Harry Rourke said he'd be in it, because he had been thinking what he would say if that runt Val O'Donoghoe turned up at the bone-yard, as good a place as any for his favourite sport of baiting human beings — and said to him, "Glad you came, Harry, because I've always wanted to know the difference between a morgue and a cemetery." Charlie East, too, badly needed a pain-killer if he was to attend a funeral for an old digger — especially if Val

O'Donoghoe was prowling around, seeking whom he might devour.

In the meantime the vicar and his boy had arrived at the cemetery, only to find that apart from the yellow flowering furze, the stunted tea-tree, the clumps of sword-grass, and the tussocks, so grey and wan, like dried-up stubble, there was no one else there. So the vicar, after robing in cassock, surplice and stole, and, lighting up a cigarette, stretched himself out on the grass and turned to the boy and said, "See where I have put the book markers, boy? In the page for the burial of the dead. My old vicar at St Peters taught me that trick. I tell you, boy, there are two moments when a clergyman's mind is likely to wander. One is when he is marrying a pretty girl: the other is when he is burying a man no one ever wanted. You take my tip, boy, and remember what I tell you. We are all fallible. You mark my words."

But the boy was far away. So the vicar tried another tack.

"Look here, boy, you're a thoughtful customer. Why don't you read what they say on these tombstones here? You can learn a lot about a people from what they put on their tombstones. You can learn a lot about their history, boy. It's the only memorial some leave. And some there be, boy, that have no memorial."

"Dad, why is it that if these people were going to heaven, they don't say anything about it on their tombstones?"

"That's a long story, boy, a very long story. You'll have to study history to find the answer to that question."

"Dad, do you think old Tug knew anything about history?"

"Tug, boy, was as free from knowledge of those things as a frog is from feathers."

"Then, how did he get on . . . how did he manage if he didn't know?"

"That, boy, is a great mystery. There are a great many mysteries in life — and here's one of them. Look, boy, here's the Thorrold family . . . swarms of them, boy. They breed children like rabbits. God spare my days, here comes the Barbour tribe. What are you blushing for, boy?"

But the boy could only manage an evasion. "I was only thinking of something," he said.

How could he tell his father that he had been having an argument for the last week about who had the more important father — Plugger Barbour's father who mended the roads, or his own father who mended souls. The blush-making thing was he was not sure he had won the argument, and was not even sure you could ever win that sort of argument. Perhaps that was another one of the mysteries in life.

Then another buggy-load arrived.

"God spare my days, boy, it's the O'Donoghoe's mob. You wait till you see Mrs Archie O'Donoghoe, boy. She's so huge they had to make a special chair for her at the picture show in Cowes, and put it in the aisle — and tell her to go quiet in her breathing because she distracted people from looking at the screen. She's got a face as red as a boiled lobster, and a voice like a rasp and a heart of gold, that's often the way, boy. The legs of one of her children are as thin as those on a diseased magpie. But take my tip, when she offers you a sandwich, look pleased, even if the crusts are as hard as iron. And, another thing, boy. Promise me faithfully you won't tell your mother about Mrs Archie's bottle of cold tea. You've got to be your father's boy today."

Within a few minutes Mrs Archie O'Donoghoe was getting herself down on the grass.

"Bloody difficult to get down when you're my size, vicar. Sorry, I didn't notice you had the boy with you. God knows what it will be like trying to get me up again. I tell Val he'll need a block and tackle."

Then she breathed, like air escaping from some huge bladder, coming first in short staccato bursts, then one steady flow, followed by a laugh like striking a chord, followed by an arpeggio — each chord pitched higher than the preceding one till she reached her limit and stopped; saying, "I always say it does a woman good to have a good laugh. It's my exercise, except what I get with Mr O'Donoghoe — sorry, vicar, I keep forgetting you've got the boy with yous. But they've got to learn one day. I must be mad wasting my water works over that bugger, old Tug. God, he was ugly — I was telling Val on the way out, I've never seen a man with an uglier mug. Better dead when they get that way, aren't they, vicar? That's what I always say. Here you are, Vicar, here's your cold tea, and don't tell me you couldn't look at it. I was telling Val I never seen a man look so happy as you after swallowing that cold tea. It makes your eyes glisten, vicar. What would the boy like to drink? Can't start him on the cold tea at his age. Who's going to fetch me the milk billy, or do I have to get myself up again? I tell you, vicar, Val and I have reared a pack of lazy loafers."

While she paused to take breath, the Reverend Hogan snatched the opportunity to raise the cup to his lips, just like he did with the chalice on Sundays.

"Anyhow, here's to your very good health, Mrs O'Donoghoe."

She beamed and raised her cup to her lips and said, "And yours, too, vicar."

This puzzled the boy because he had never seen ladies do quite that when they were drinking tea with his mother in the sitting-room at the vicarage. Those ladies looked as though they were straining the tea through their teeth, while here his father gulped his down with one huge swallow . . . which was not what his mother had told him was good manners. Then his father looked for a moment as though he had tasted something very unpleasant, like epsom salts or castor oil or cascara, and yet the next moment a wonderful smile spread right over his face and he said something even more astonishing.

"That's better," he said.

Perhaps he should ask his father if he could have some of that cold tea which made him look so pleased.

"Do you think I could have some of your cold tea, Daddy . . . it seems to make you so happy?"

"Take my tip, boy, and stick to the milk. It's much better for you."

But when the boy replied that he had never seen anyone drink more than two glasses of milk, but he had once seen his father and uncle Herman take six glasses each of cold tea, Mrs O'Donoghoe giggled and said, "By God, vicar, that's rich." And the Reverend Mr Hogan looked so pleased the boy thought for a moment his father was going to cry, as he put his arm round him just like the way he had put his arm round Uncle

Herman when they had walked to the front gate together after six glasses of cold tea.

"Anyone can see he's his father's boy," he said.

To which Mrs Archie retorted, just managing to get it out before another fit of laughing shook her whole body, "By God, vicar, you don't half kid yourself, do you?"

After which she regained her composure and said, "Thank God for that. I thought for a moment, vicar, you were going to give me a fit of me hysterics."

Then, using her arms like two powerful stays to keep erect the huge tent of herself, she nodded towards the spot where her husband Val had squatted down and said, "I don't like the way that Val is putting them away up there. I tell you, vicar, it's bloody ominous, that's what I call it, bloody ominous. If he gets many more under his belt before you do your own little act over poor old Tug, I'm warning you, vicar, there's going to be a lot of those filthy jokes about Queenie Rourke as the local morgue. And when Val's finished playing with Harry like boys with butterfly wings, he'll still have enough of the devil in him to start needling Charlie East about why he never shouldered a rifle with his cobbers in the war. After a few drinks, vicar, my Val can get bloody vicious."

"He's not all that bad, your Val. You know my dear old mother used to tell me, when she was alive, Mrs O'Donoghoe, that God had planted some good in all of us."

"All I can say is that judging by my Val, when he's got a few drinks under his belt, God's been unemployed for a mighty long time."

She tore up some grass near her as though to find relief in the angry gesture, because life had taught her that no matter how much she and all the other people she knew might want to stop her Val, there was just nothing they could do about it, and if it wasn't that the vicar was such a good sort, what with his jokes and all his stories ("Listen, Mrs O'Donoghoe, you're going to like this story . . . I always think about you when I'm telling this one") and how could a woman resist him when he was as sweet as that, she'd give him a piece of her mind about all this talk about us all becoming meek and mild. If God loved us all the way the vicar said, how in the hell did he come to make such a bloody bloomer as to make her Val, who spent all his time scaring the daylights out of his own kids, and when he wasn't doing that, hurting Harry Rourke about his wife being a whore, the local bike, or tormenting Charlie East for showing his tail during the war and putting round that cock and bull story about tossing a coin. I've seen the bugger tie his own kid up to a tree of a Sunday and whip him till he dropped. . . . The person who made him must have had a bloody funny sense of humour. And how did I ever make such a bloody bloomer as to marry the bugger?

Just as she was wondering whether to give the vicar a piece of her mind, the buggy carrying Harry Rourke, Charlie East and Billy Gossop came into sight. Behind them came the dray carrying old Tug's coffin — a plain deal box with the Australian flag draped over it as a tribute to an old digger. Old Sam Matthews, who made a few bob every now and then knocking up a coffin for those who were too poor or too stingy to pay a funeral director, was walking with appropriate dignity behind the dray, his black suit, black tie, and stiff butterfly collar adding an air of solemnity, perhaps of pathos, to the cortège bearing old Tug over the last stages of his earthly pilgrimage.

The vicar knelt down right beside Mrs O'Donoghoe and squeezed her left arm gently and whispered, "Promise me you'll see the boy doesn't hear the thud of the clods on the coffin. He mustn't hear it, do you hear, he mustn't hear it."

"What's so bloody special about clods of earth thuddin' on wood?"

The boy noticed that all the gaiety and the laughter were disappearing like thistle-down before the wind. Suddenly everyone began to talk in whispers and to tread softly. Mrs Archie heaved herself up and gathered all the children together. The women drew apart from the men just as the boy saw his father shake Val O'Donoghoe warmly by the hand and say, "It's awfully good of you to find time to join us in saying goodbye to old Tug."

The boy looked the other way, just as he did when his father asked him to hold a chook while he chopped its head off, ("I was like you once, boy, but you'll get used to it. You'll even love it one day, boy, you'll see") but as the gust of disgust and dismay began to emerge as words in the head — so this is being all things to all men — Mrs O'Donoghoe, a cheery soul if ever there was one, laughed him out of it:

"How about a game with me and the kids while yer dad buries old Tug?"

The men began to form their own knot round the huge hole in the ground. Val O'Donoghoe, rather a weedy man for a flogger of children, his suit hanging as loosely over his body as his lower lip to his chin, his mouth, as usual in the smiling position, though dead eyes belied what the mouth was saying, broke the silence with one of those remarks he sometimes made when the smile had temporarily vanished off his face.

"Well, anyhow, with Bob Barbour, Henry Rourke, Billy Gossop and myself, at least there are four old diggers here to carry an old digger to his last resting place."

Charlie East let drop into the silence the one protest he ever allowed himself:

"Jesus Christ."

Billy Gossop squeezed Charlie's arm just as the vicar, who had taken up a position at one of the narrow sides of the grave, turned his head round to the five of them and smiled tenderly as though remembering suddenly that his blessed Lord had had compassion on the multitude. He began to recite the words, "I am the resurrection and the life, saith the Lord: he that believeth in me, though he were dead, yet shall he live: and whosoever liveth and believeth in me shall never die."

The words had an extraordinary effect on the vicar: he felt lifted up, he felt as though he had the power to bring all manner of men unto him: a few minutes earlier he had winced inwardly at the very thought of using any words at all about one of God's creatures who for some mysterious reason had become an abomination in the sight of man. Now he was transformed: he felt like that man to whom the voice of God had said, "Prophesy".

He decided the time had come to testify to God's world. It might mean very little to some of them, but that Billy Gossop was a deep one on whom the words would not be altogether lost. He would follow the Rubric in the *Book of Common Prayer* — "After they are come unto the church, shall be read one or more of these Psalms following." He read slowly those words which had comforted him in his days of anguish, "I held my tongue, and spake nothing: I held silence", and hesitated because he knew that that holding of his tongue was just what he had never been able to achieve in life. He had sent up his great cry of anguish — and that was why he had been sent to this God-forsaken island to care for the souls of people like old Tug and Val O'Donoghoe. Then he continued,

"*For man walketh in a vain shadow and disquieteth himself in vain.*

Make me not a rebuke unto the foolish

Thou makest his beauty to consume away, like as it were a moth fretting a garment

For I am a stranger with thee: and a sojourner, as all my fathers were."

He wondered whether he should stop for a moment, and say to them, "And we are all strangers to each other", but decided not to, because the next verse said all that needed to be said about life, that simple cry to God from all his creatures who felt they had been punished enough, but knew the hounding would go on until the day they died.

"*O spare me a little, that I may recover my strength: before I go hence, and be no more seen.*"

And not even a ripple appeared on Harry Rourke's face when he heard the words of that desperate petition. A faint glimmer of hope appeared in Charlie East's eyes, shaded though they were by the huge sockets, and the bushy eyebrows, like old tussocks flattened by the wind on the top of a cliff. He looked as though it was a comfort to him to know there had been a man who wanted to be spared from being haunted and hunted by something from his past, something he had not even wished to happen, something like a tossing of a coin which had fallen the wrong way and given low bastards like Val O'Donoghoe just the chance they had been looking for to get their fangs into him.

The vicar came to that part of the service for the burial of the dead where the priest and those present recite the one prayer Christ had commanded all men to use, and said "Our Father"; but only Val O'Donoghoe and Billy Gossop had joined in by the time he got to "Thy will be done on earth". God's world had given Val plenty of opportunities for his sport with humanity. "It'll do me, mate," he was fond of saying. As for Billy Gossop, as he just could not see how it could ever be any different, he felt he might just as well say "Thy will be done". God's will wouldn't do any harm, and there was always the chance it might do some good. Then the vicar, sensing the drift in their minds, decided not to say the words:

"Rest eternal grant unto them."

That was all very well: everyone knew that yearning. The trouble was what came after.

"And let light perpetual shine upon them."

Who would want old Tug to be lit up — either literally or metaphorically? So he recited the words of the closing prayer, hoping those who had come to mourn might not be tempted to laugh at God's sense of the fitness of things:

"We give thee hearty thanks for that it hath pleased thee to deliver this our brother out of the miseries of this sinful world."

And Billy Gossop was astonished. Does that mean, he asked himself, that God is on the side of humanity? The others were puzzled — except for Val O'Donoghoe who was beginning to think it was an awfully long time since he had had a "snort" from that bottle which made him feel towards Charlie East like a whippet to a juicy young rabbit.

Billy Gossop, never a man to waste much time over questions no man could answer, was thinking it was really very nice of the vicar to get so worked up saying goodbye to a slobbering bastard like old Tug.

As the grave-digger shovelled in the sods, which, sure enough, thudded on the lid, just as the vicar had predicted they would, the boy plucked his father's cassock and asked plaintively, "When are we going home?"

But the vicar rebuked him gently. "Remember, boy, what our Saviour taught us: "Blessed are they that mourn."

Then, to the boy's eyes, the adults seemed to go all silly. He heard Billy Gossop say, "He wasn't such a bad old bugger really."

His own father then said, "As my dear old mother used to say, he meant well."

To which Val O'Donoghoe said, lifting his eyes for once off the ground, "He certainly meant well to a jug of beer."

They all laughed. Then Mrs O'Donoghoe waddled up to the grave-side, puffing and panting as she always did after the slightest movement, face as red as ever, but genial and laughing, as though life for her was one huge joke, and said, "How about another cup of cold tea, vicar, before you set out for Cowes?"

"You took the words out of my mouth, Mrs O'Donoghoe."

She shook with laughter, the food-stained, drink-stained black silk dress, which she had worn first when her own mother had passed on, showing more of her white shimmy through the slits at the waist which had appeared to allow for her expansion since those early middle years, the face reddening with the pleasure of the giver.

"By God, Mrs O'Donoghoe," the vicar said, "you'll burst one day, and they'll pick up little bits of you all over the island. And then we will mourn — that is, all those that thirst."

O'Donoghoe said, "I hope you kept a drop at the bottom of the bottle for your old pal Val."

After Mrs O'Donoghoe had gone back to the place where the children were sitting watching with mingled wonder and contempt at the man's world, Billy Gossop said, "Now you've all got something in your cups, let's drink to our departed friend, old Tug."

For a brief moment it seemed to the boy that they were all much more kindly to each other. It was like one of those moments when the sea flattened out in between winds. Billy Gossop put his arm first round Harry Rourke, and then round Charlie East. Even Val O'Donoghoe smiled in a way which was not a prelude to hurting someone. To the boy it all seemed so different from what happened when the women in the Ladies' Guild in Cowes drank tea with his mother, that he wondered if perhaps when they were going home together he might risk asking his father why women were so different from men . . . only he was afraid the question would only make his father start to clown again and recite with dignity, "Male and female created He them, boy", or, worse still, put his father into one of those terrible moods when, flicking words like Val O'Donoghoe flicking a whip in front of a boy's face, he would say, "There's no giving in marriage on the resurrection morning, boy — Humanity, boy, has friends in Heaven, even if it has few on earth," and then look awfully pleased with himself, just as the boy felt so miserable.

For the moment, thank God, his father, like all the other men, was being very gentle with both man and beast. As his father backed old Ginger between the shafts, he patted her rump tenderly and then tickled her in a friendly way on the nose, while Billy Gossop asked him how much he wanted for his trouble. And his father said it had been no trouble at all, that it had been a real pleasure and an honour to be with them, and they could use some of the money by having a drink on him at the bar of the Phillip Island Hotel when they got back to Cowes. Then Billy Gossop repeated what he had already said at the grave-side, that old Tug was not such a bad bugger really, except when he got drunk, but then we were all troublesome when we were drunk, weren't we vicar? And he added, "At least he knew the island in the days before the locusts descended on it."

The boy was so astonished when his father looked wise and said that in his experience locusts always ate "young grass, Mr Gossop, if you see what I mean", that he could not help himself saying, "But last Sunday night after church, Dad, you told that judge from Melbourne that visitors would be the making of the island."

That broke the spell. The vicar said he would have to be moving or the wife would be wondering what he was up to, and away they went in silence down the long hill from the cemetery till the vicar turned to the boy and said, "How many times, boy, must I tell you not to let the parishioners know what I think?"

The boy curled up in his corner of the seat.

"Now don't blabber, boy. I know you meant well. But when you get to my age, boy, you'll understand why our Saviour commanded his disciples to tell no man anything, not even about his good deeds. I tell you, boy, never let anyone know what you're thinking. You take my tip, boy."

As the father spoke, the boy was wondering why at one moment there was gentleness and at another there was this. And he began to think of the sea at the blow-hole at the

Nobbies and to say to himself, "It does not last for long — it's as brief as a smooth sea at the blow-hole."

By the time they reached the sand patch on the way back to Cowes, darkness had descended on them. The boy watched in wonder as the moon, so pale in the sky by day, now so white, darted in and out of the clouds tipping their edges with silver. As it disappeared behind cloud again, darkness enveloped them, and then as it came out of the other side of the cloud it bathed them all in light, his father, old Ginger, the jinker and the gum-trees. When they moved faster, the moon always seemed to keep up with them. Coming out from behind a cloud, it never gained on them when old Ginger walked, and never dropped behind when old Ginger got a move on.

Feeling that his father's disapproval had vanished into thin air, and had been replaced by something of what he himself was feeling — that there was something special about two bodies, two dark shapes swaying there in the moonlight with not a sound except the dull roar of the sea in the Strait ("That, boy, will go on through all eternity. You mark my words") and the rhythmic thud of old Ginger's hooves on the sand — and thinking too that as there was no one to hear them or spy on them, except perhaps God, who must surely understand, because no one else ever did understand, except occasionally his father (unlike his mother, who only wanted to change him, or his brother, who only wanted to laugh and tell others what a peculiar brother he had) he decided to put a question to his father. After all, his father never put on a frown when he asked him about the things he was thinking about.

When he said to his father, "Dad, do you mind if I ask you something?" he put his arm round him and said friendly, trusting, on-coming, "ask me anything you like, boy."

"Do you think God's the same size as the world?"

"God spare my days, boy, what on earth put that idea in your head?"

"Because, dad, if He was the same size as the world, then He wouldn't be able to move."

For the boy, the impotence of God was something deeply pleasing. The God he heard about on Sundays reminded him of those bullies at school who ordered him to dive off a high rock into the sea, and when he could not or would not, being afraid, they twisted his arm for breaking their commandment. It was not that he wanted to punish them, or hurt them for what they had done to him. He just wanted all bullies — including God, and the boys at school — in a position where they could not hurt him any more.

For his father it was quite different. For him God was his refuge, his harbour on which his ship would one day ride after being tossed by the terrible oceans of life. The Reverend Mr Hogan had come to the conclusion there was no point in looking to man for the satisfactions he craved. Like his Saviour, he had been once in the world but the world had known him not. So the Reverend Mr Hogan, being impotent to bend the world to his will, was beginning to feel like a man who had performed his act on the stage of life, and found, to his ever-lasting chagrin, that the audience he had so desperately wished to reach, had booed him off that part of the stage where he wanted to stand. That was what had drawn him to God — the one who could and would put right all those things men never did anything about. God was a fixer, who made everything come right in the end — the one who patched up humanity's blunders.

The longer he lived, the more he had been tempted to say to himself, "God's taking an awful long time to do anything about it." Here on this God-forsaken island, Val O'Donoghoe, it was said, tied his boy to a tree and whipped him until the blood ran, and the ants swarmed round the foot of the tree, and neither God nor man did anything about it. He could only conclude, again, that was the sort of thing Christ had had in mind when He had told his disciples to let the tares grow with the wheat. But how could he tell simple chicory farmers who did not earn enough in a year to give their families a decent feed, and if it were not for the fish and rabbits they would probably starve, that the Heavenly Father was going to do something about it at humanity's harvest time, when God, the great reaper, gathered his crop into the barn — or as they called it on the island, into the kiln.

Yet, here in this white moonlight which softened the daytime sense of harshness and desolation on the wind-swept island, pounded as it had been by those huge seas from the south ever since God had made his world, it gave him a twinge to think the boy, too, had already been driven to put God up for scanning. So, instead of replying, instead of enjoying the joke as the boy had hoped, for what more pleasing conceit was there for their sort than to think of the whippers of mankind not even able to move, he flicked old Ginger so hard on the rump and said to the boy, "When you get married, boy, always arrive on time, otherwise they'll start to talk about broken promises."

When the horse responded, not with a lively trot but with a stumble, the father took the whip again out of its stand, stood bolt upright, using the reins to steady his swaying, reeling body and cracked the whip so hard between the horse's upright ears that old Ginger hollered out loud and jerked into a sullen trot, casting back fearful glances behind her to see whether there was more where that came from. The father turned in triumph to the boy: "What am I always telling you, boy? There's nothing like a good flick of the whip between the ears to teach a horse not to stumble. It takes some doing, let me tell you, boy."

The boy knew his father had to stop the stumble. The Saviour had said something about it: what was it? Something like woe unto that man who caused the least of the little ones to fall into the pit. He was not sure if he was remembering it correctly: he never did, and that was one of his troubles in life. But if only his father had not thrashed old Ginger with the whip, then the jinker would not career madly into the black night, with the horses legs like scissors, hacking a way through the darkness. The silence, everywhere except for the swishing of the air past them, the weak shadows cast by the light on the jinker, all helped to stir up once again inside him that source of his private terror. Was not the earth itself, on which they all lived, like the jinker on which he and his father were riding . . . hurtling into a great darkness, out of nowhere into nowhere? So, try as he did never to let that fear come up from inside him so that other people would ask what on earth was the matter with him, a little cry of alarm escaped from him which caused the father to put his left arm around him and encourage him to rest his head on his father's breast, as though it were a nest of swansdown where he could hide.

"If you're feeling windy or scary, boy," his father said gently, "close your eyes tight."

Fearing lest any confession that it was not what he could see that was troubling, but something else, something inside him, would certainly give his father the chance once again to pontificate and say, "What am I always telling you, boy? It's what goes on inside a man that leads him to destruction," the boy refrained, and turned away from his father just enough to stir up in his parent the idea that here he was once again stretching out his arms, and being rejected. He knew, of course, that his Saviour had been rejected by men. But that was different. He wanted man's regard: that was why he was alway stretching out his arms, reaching, as it were, for something and not finding anything there.

Ever since the Reverend Hogan had come to the island, Charlie East, who had caught a ten pound blue-nose in a deep hole on the left of the Nobbies, was always promising to take him to the right-hand side of the Pyramid. "I think you'd be safe there, Mr Hogan, if we can get you there on a day when a north-easter is blowing. It doesn't happen very often, but, by jingo when it does, I can guarantee you a sugar-bag full of those deep-sea leather-jackets. You'll need a copper-wire lead, vicar, or the beggars will bite through your line." But whenever the vicar peered over the cliff at the Pyramid Rock, huge waves, streaked with white foam, thumped all day on that rock below which Charlie East had told him the deep-sea leatherjohnnies were feeding. He had to be content with fishing on the lee side of Pyramid Rock where only the green parrot fish his wife would not even bother to cook, sucked away at his bait. As he stood there in his quiet haven, hearing the boom and crash of the sea on the rocks where the big fish lay, he began to wonder at times whether it was to be his fate in life to dream of hooking a "big beauty" while pulling in the Tom Tiddlers.

It was the same with the cricket. There, again, there was that gap between desire and capacity. His favourite shot was the late-cut. ("Watch me, boy, while I show you my late-cut. Are you watching, boy? See how the right eye is right over the ball so that if it fell out it would fall on the ball. Then, boy, you give the flick of the wrist. Are you watching, boy? I can tell you,

25

boy, many's the time I have stood at the crease and watched the ball speed to the pickets on the Petersham oval like greased lightning.") But here at Cowes, on the matting wicket, the ball never rose to the right height, the bat was never the right weight, the handle was always too long ("That's another thing I can tell you, boy, all graceful cricketers use a short handle. Take Charlie McCartney as an example of what I am telling you.") But here if the flick of the wrist worked, the ball stopped in the long grass about ten yards from his bat. Every Saturday afternoon he padded up, pulled on his batting gloves, the left glove first just for luck, donned his Petersham cap, and walked out to open the innings for Cowes with another young fellow who had walked to the wicket with one brown pad (trust him to pick a brown pad) so badly strapped that he would take it off, throw it back to the pavilion, shouting out, "Here, take this bloody thing, will you! What bloody use is it anyway?" This lout would stand there in his collarless shirt, dark trousers held up by braces made out of old bridle leather, grey felt hat tilted back so that he could see the yonnie coming towards him, take a step towards the square-leg umpire before the bowler delivered the ball, and swoosh at it, cross-bat mind you, but by sheer physical strength he would send the ball a long way in the air. By these cow-shots — and that's what they were, cow-shots — this galoot mustered twenty or thirty while he had to be content with a one from a delicate leg glance and then go out trying to force things a bit after the captain sent out a message asking the vicar whether he would mind shaking a leg.

Over afternoon tea, one of the women from the Ladies' Committee would listen to his story when he took her aside, and told her that what he missed here most of all was the chance to play the glance and the late-cut. There had been that terrible day when one of the locals, who had a considerable skill in raising a laugh by deliberate rudeness, said to him as they were about to go back on the field, "It's runs that count here, vicar, not fancy strokes. Keep your fancy strokes for when you're going out with the ladies." They had all laughed so hard he had told his wife that he was finished with cricket, but she had reminded him that Mr Lamble liked him to play every Saturday, as it was good for the offertory on Sundays. So he thought better of it and continued to play every Saturday and practised the late-cut in front of the long mirror in the wardrobe in his bedroom where he also kept his bottle of "cold tea", determined he'd show those whippersnappers what cricket was really like.

But each Saturday it was the same. The immaculate straight bat ("A bat, boy, is like the gate leading to eternal life: it must be straight") and the flick of the wrist brought him a paltry single at the end of thirty minutes of what he called stylishness and the locals called "frigging around". Then, when the message came out to get a wriggle on, he took a dip, up the ball soared, and some galoot, cupping his hands above his head, held the catch. Out he would have to go and wait for that precious moment when that woman with a sweet face would spare the time to hear what he was like in his Petersham days and how he did not mind telling her that on a turf wicket these cow-yard batsmen would not last a minute. There he was Saturday after Saturday, he who had been one of the most promising batsmen in grade cricket in Sydney, thirsting for one word of praise from a wife of a poverty-stricken chickory farmer on a wind-swept God-forsaken island surrounded by a hostile sea which went on roaring and roaring till the end of the world and would roar again in the life of the world to come, like the uproar in his own soul.

As he sat there in the jinker with the boy, it seemed such a long time ago that he had first listened in wonder to the claims of what God could do. He remembered that day when he had gone as a boy to St Andrew's Cathedral in Sydney and heard the sopranos, altos, tenors and basses on one side of the choir stalls whisper the words, "Thou stillest the raging of the waters", and then the sopranos, altos, tenors and basses on the other side had replied, "And Thou stillest the madness of the people", and he had begun to cry for joy to hear that there was someone who could tame or subdue what terrified him most in life — the raging of the sea and the madness of the people.

The locals were always telling him to wait for the day when there were no white horses on McHaffy's Reef, but in the few months he had lived on the island white horses swirled round the reef every day. He could even see them on moonlight nights, white shapes in the surrounding blackness mocking the secret longings of his soul. He knew the ocean in all its moods, knew it in those still autumn days when a gentle southerly brought in a fine curtain of spray off the southern ocean and dropped it on the wizened tea tree, the stunted tussocks and the pig-face on the cliff edge. He knew it in its frolicsome moods, when it rushed into the gutters which it had cut into the rocks, and gambolled around like one possessed, before rushing out again. He knew it in its more menacing and noisy moods, when it pounded and crashed relentlessly on the rocks. He knew all the changes of colours in the water, from the black under the rockface after sun-down, to the brilliant blue and the blobs of gold on the rare cloudless days. He knew the bottle green of a giant comber off Pyramid Rock and the dirty, foamy water of a winter storm which crumpled the line of the ocean on the horizon. That ocean went on hissing, like water falling on hot metal, and thumping and heaving and dropping, and would go on heaving and dropping until that resurrection morning when, according to God's promises, it was going to give up its dead. Perhaps then at last it would be quiet, when it had spewed up all human filth.

There had been a time when he would have been ashamed to refer to mankind as filth. In the days when he was young it had all seemed so clear, for then his eye was single. He had responded to Christ's promise that He had come that men might have life and have it more abundantly. He had come to this island when his heart was hot with the idea that Christ was mankind's fairy godmother who would make everything come right in the end. Then one Sunday after the service at Ventnor Annie East had told him she must hurry on home in case her nipper was taken queer again while she was away . . . and had taken the twelve-gauge gun again and told his sister Bella she'd been playing up again with that O'Rourke boy, chasing each other bare in the tea-tree, and had ordered her to take off all her clothes and walk backwards into Cowes. And when Annie East had asked him whether perhaps it was because she had been such a sinner that God had punished her, he could not tell her that God was sending her this suffering to prepare her to enter in at the strait gate.

Why was it that for a man whose message was about love, he spent so much time being angry? Why had he been visited with "bitterness of soul"? There were those nightmare scenes in the local school when he wanted so much to tell the least of the little ones about the kingdom of God but ended up, to his chagrin, acting like a vulgar buffoon. That teacher fellow, that man Gwillim, a bit of a Welsh bolshie if ever there was one, insisted on staying in the classroom, saying it was his school after all and he had a right to hear what the children were told; adding rudely, "I've never had much time myself for medieval dirt, Mr Hogan. I became a teacher because I wanted a generation of young Australians to grow up without their minds poisoned by all that talk about foulness. I don't want my children to beat their breasts and say, 'Lord, I am not worthy'. I don't want them to sing:

> *Foul I to the fountain fly,*
> *Wash me, Saviour, or I die."*

Why was it that he could not even convince a State School teacher on a God-forsaken island of that truth to which he had dedicated his whole life? Perhaps that was why he carried on like a buffoon when it was his turn to take them for scripture? He shuddered inwardly as the picture of himself in front of the class flickered before his mind's eye.

"Now, all eyes on me. . . . Are you watching, Curly? . . . What's your name? My dear old mother taught me to love curly-headed boys." (Those terrible titters whenever he lapsed in that way.) "What's your first duty on Sunday?" And the reply he had taught the children to make — "Go to church." . . . "How many of you went to church on Sunday? Now, don't be afraid to put your hands up. So far I can only count four. I wonder how many of you went swimming on Sunday. This time I count thirty-five at least."

This was followed by a loud guffaw from behind him. He had swung round in time to see that Gwillim fellow winking at the older girls in the front seat. So he had decided to teach Gwillim what was what. ("I can tell you, boy, that when I tell one of the stories from the New Testament you can hear a pin drop.") Their little eyes had followed him all round the

29

room as he had told them the story of the good Samaritan, only at the end Colin Twyrold had spoiled it all by asking what was so special about being nice to a fellow who had been donged on the nut?

"If you really want to know, Colin, then I'll tell you. The man who told that story was the son of God. I'm sure of it, Colin, I'm as sure of it as I am that I am standing here in front of you."

The little beggars had tittered nervously, and then that fellow Gwillim had told them to get out their arithmetic books, and he would teach them something they might find handy.

He knew what his "me" was. It was what was going to be left of him on the resurrection morning, when he had discarded his earthly selves, those persons he had created to protect himself against the world and the world against him. Then he would no longer need to be a clown, or a buffoon, or wound people who had hurt him, or put on the quelling look. That huge pack he had carried round the world would fall off him. He would stand there with his "me" before his God and He, God, would not forgive him, because he, the Reverend Hogan, God's buffoon of the Cowes State School, and one time Falstaff of Moore College (a man played many parts in life, thank God) was not looking to God for forgiveness. God would do what no man had ever done for him. He would not admire or applaud or condemn: God would like his "me" — and this no man had ever done. There must be somebody, somewhere, who would like his "me" — not the wit, the clown, the story-teller, or the crusher.

As the horse whinnied with delight on seeing the vicarage gate, a new thought began to take shape in his mind. If all the striving, the strutting, and the fretting had only left him with what Job called "bitterness of soul", or had taught him what the Psalmist meant by the words that man "disquieteth himself in vain", then maybe there was peace in acceptance. And he began to experience a new tenderness towards Billy Gossop who lives alone because for him there could not be another, for the school-teacher Gwillim, who, like Prometheus, believed in planting "blind hopes" to stop mortals forseeing the doom of death. The anger and the loathing had evaporated. He even came to accept Lamble with his greed and his vision seeing the treasure a man could lay up for himself on earth by exploiting the island as a tourist resort. Yes, and even that no-hoper, the State Governor, who used to tell the chicory farmers they ought to fatten their sheep and their cattle by sowing English grasses; and Charlie East, who had to live with his guilt as all men must live with their past; and Harry Rourke, to whom a woman had done great evil, just as Alexander the coppersmith had done great evil to the apostle Paul; and Val O'Donoghoe, who would not stop tormenting his own kind; and that huge mountain of flesh, that woman with a face as red as a beetroot, and no teeth, and a mouth which looked as though she was always sucking in air, who had to live with a man who could not stop. . . .

In the bar of the Phillip Island Hotel, while the Reverend Hogan was thus musing, Harry Rourke, Charlie East and Billy Gossop were rapidly approaching that state of unsteadiness where they could minister comfort to each other without any embarrassment. They stood there, Billy with his back to the wall, Harry resting his left hand on the bar rail, and Charlie resting his right hand on it. For the most part they were silent. A grunt, they had found, did more justice to their own brand of despair than thousands of words. After a long silence and much vacant staring, Billy began to laugh, not with pleasure, but with a noise suggesting savage indignation.

Charlie East asked him quietly, "Here, what's biting you?"

"I was thinking of those words in the service about old Tug being in sure and certain hope of resurrection to eternal life. By God, that's rich. If we can't face the truth about the dead, how are we ever going to face the truth about the living?"

Discovery

EVERY time Charles Hogan and his elder brother behaved outrageously their mother would cry in despair, "I don't know what I'm going to do with you boys. Sometimes I wish I could send you to a good boarding school. At least it would make men of you." So it stood in their lives as a threat, a fate to be dreaded, as well as something outside the field of the possible — for as a family they belonged to the genteel poor. Then one day in November of 1927 Charles won a scholarship to Batman Grammar School. A bachelor uncle in New Zealand, who still retained some of the wealth which all other members of the family had squandered so wantonly, or lost as mysteriously in the bank crash of the 1890s, came to the rescue with a promise to pay for the elder brother so long as Charles held his scholarship. And Mrs Hogan began to tell all who were prepared to listen that her Charles had won a scholarship. That was the first discovery, this metamorphosis of the prison-house, where they were to be flogged into being men, into a place of honour, a place which all coveted but few could achieve.

So one day in February of 1928 with the bags strapped on to

the running-board of a Morris roadster (they used rope because leather was far too expensive for a family of their limited means), with Mr and Mrs Hogan in the front seat, and Charles and his brother in the dicky seat, they set out from Belgrave for the long drive to Melbourne; where, with tears in her eyes, and a rather smothering, mothering embrace, and that puzzling use of her two themes, ". . . it will make a man of you, dear, it will make a man of you," and, ". . . if you only knew how proud we all are of you," she and her husband, who contented himself with an enigmatic "Good luck to you, boy," adding a "You'll need it," were off; and Hogan and his brother walked away from the car, away from the world they had known, away from the friends of their childhood, away from those with whom they had fished and trapped rabbits, and had been both betrayers and betrayed, walked away from all that into a new world. Feeling like men about to explore a new world, and, like them, tempted to rush back to the familiar, to what they knew, they looked back towards the car; but that symbol of their early world had disappeared. Before them were huge iron gates through which they walked and then down some steps and over a brick quadrangle, and through a door, and into a great darkness.

Everything that happened over the next few weeks was, for Charles, like those pictures in the mind during a high fever, like those grotesque distortions of life pictures, as it were, which never seemed to fall into focus. In the rare moments when the fever left him, he did not feel that he could talk about what was happening to him, because it was too shameful and humiliating to let anyone know that any other person would do such things to him. There was that moment, for example, when he saw a wave of pleasure sweep over the face of the assistant chaplain when he showed the boy with whom he was to play tennis that they would be using new balls — off-white, fluffy, bouncy balls and not those smooth-surfaced, drunken-flighted ones which he could afford. What was the meaning of that? Why was that the one thing which could make the assistant chaplain become warm and friendly? Yet if he, Charles, so much as smiled at the assistant chaplain, he was greeted with a look of lofty disdain.

Within a few weeks, too, it seemed to Charles that the school was not at all concerned with what it claimed to be its concern. Every Sunday in chapel they all went down on their knees and asked that the paths of true learning might ever flourish and abound. Yet for the other six days of the week they seemed to be concerned with something quite different. Masters seemed to become much more angry if a boy spoke to them with hands in pocket than if he misconstrued a passage of Latin prose: one master, for example, had raged horribly in the first week when a boy from the country wore a blue shirt with a white collar. Why was that? And yet every time he tried to puzzle this out, the answer eluded him.

He was just as puzzled by the behaviour of the boys to each other, puzzled, that is, by what the few at the top were inflicting on all the rest. For here again, as far as he could see, they were not concerned with achievement, with subduing the passions, with either truth or beauty (he did not, of course, use such words at that time) or with the quest of the greatest and the best in their civilization and their religion. What was very puzzling, neither the aspiration to be like that precious One, nor the hope that one day, in some future time and place, there would be a happy issue out of all afflictions for the faithful servants of Christ, seemed to touch them at all.

What they seemed driven to achieve, what was for them the greatest good, was not that Christ figure, not that Greek ideal of "know thyself", but a much more limited objective, something much less exciting, though, in its own way, quite terrifying, for they seemed to be driven on by some desperate passion to see that all boys had the same haircuts, thought the same thoughts, and were "true to our dark blue". Within the first few weeks disturbing stories were passed on from boy to boy about what happened to those who did not conform. It took Charles a fortnight to find out that if you used a brush-back, wore the hair long, or horror of horrors, had a *nana* haircut, *they*, the ones in charge of behaviour, sent for you in the middle of the night, and belted you with towels till you promised not to offend again.

Try as he would, he could make no progress in discovering how he should think. The only times he had let slip what was in his mind in front of one of *them* had left a wound in his memory. Once he was in one of his cheeky, indeed one of his impish moods, and was staring fondly at the plate of peaches and cream which one of *them* had bought as an extra — an antidote to the never-ending potatoes, stew, and sago pudding — hoping for a slice, for he had seen other boys in his group win a slice, and a peach, and some cream, and some of the juice, by just being nice. So when one of *them* asked him sharply, "What are you staring at, *ickle man*?" he replied with a toss of the head, "I was wondering whether you would find that anticipation was a greater joy than realization." But *he*, the one of *them*, was not amused, nor, for that matter, was the rest of the table. *He* snapped, "Our ickle man's quite a show-off." Over the next few weeks Charles made many attempts to win the regard of the same boy, but every move always ended in the hot flush of humiliation and defeat.

So by the time Easter came (it was very late that year) he was beginning to wear a puzzled, anxious look on his face, and when May came soon after, with the leaves from the plane-trees rotting in the dungy, springy earth on the Domain, he began to wear a mask, to try to make sure that the face did not, even by the movement of a single muscle, betray to the outside world what was going on within. He began to withdraw more and more, to find in solitude the one priceless treasure of never being tormented by anyone except his own thoughts in which, by the simplest act of the will, he could preserve uninterrupted pictures of delight.

It was not that the outside world had ceased to beckon to him, or to offer him moments of pleasure. Sometimes when the choir sang a verse from the Psalms, such as "Lord, I am not high-minded, I have no proud looks," the tears would come to his eyes, and his throat would be so constricted that for a moment it was as though he could not talk. It was the same at nightfall when darkness descended over all the land, and just before the stars came out, a luminous light suffused the edges of the sky, and the wind stopped nudging the trees, and silence descended, a great hush, during which the fever and the fret of the world seemed also to be still. For a moment neither man nor beast was tormenting the other, and he used to think then of that other darkness inside him, that sensing of a great mystery at the heart of things. In the great hush, there was a promise that one day he might find an answer to it; a promise that one day he might be able to live with it, and find the strength to put up with what went on in the world, as though all humiliations, cruelties and torments were insignificant and trivial beside such a mystery.

The odd thing was he could not speak to anyone about the things that really mattered. So there had to be two lives: this secret life, in which he was like one of the ancient mariners, setting out on a voyage of discovery of the human heart, having taken a vow not to tell anyone what he found, and that other life, that life of living with the other boys where the cunning needed to evade trouble was always warring with some darker passion — with another voice inside him which drove him recklessly on to contests with those who wanted all boys to think little and alike.

By May, he used to say years later, he had stumbled on the secret that he who wishes to enjoy the world must travel alone. He walked to the boat races alone that year. It may be that was one of those ironies of chance — this alienation from the other boys in his year, who were surprised to find that he was one of the very few who ever comforted them when they were in trouble. They were not to know that he already believed there could be no sorrow like unto his sorrow, as though loving kindness was all that human beings had to put between themselves and those blows they were quite impotent to stop raining on them from our coming hither until our going hence.

Whatever the reason, he walked alone that year to the boat-races, walked alone along those asphalt paths on the edge of the Domain, at times shamed into some sense of inferiority by his failure to be with the others, and at other times buoyed up by some feeling of superiority, of being marked out, singled out from the others for some purpose, some calling which, at that time, he could but dimly perceive. When he arrived at the river bank he was glad he had come alone, because anyone else would only have got in the way of what he was about to explore. A great tide of people was moving towards the finishing post for the races. There, small knots of boys wearing the same distinctively coloured caps, formed themselves into a ring and began to chant, as they jumped up and down:

> *Who are we?*
> *Can't you guess?*
> *We're the boys of the G.G.S.!*

Another group immediately began to form and bob up and down, shouting:

> *Get your boat and lift her,*
> *Take your oars and shift her,*

throwing their caps in the air in a last moment of frenzy when they shouted, *"Wesley, Wesley, Ra, Ra, Ra."* Then the boys from his own school formed their ring and began to sing:

> *Row the race, boys, swing together,*
> *Sinews tough as cords of leather,*
> *Strong yet light upon the feather,*
> *Lift her, make her go!*

And he would have joined in with them — one part of him urged, "Have a go — surrender . . . lose yourself with your own" — but another side of him said that to do so would mean identifying oneself with one side, becoming part of the show, and so ceasing to be an observer of life. What he wanted then most passionately was to see it all, to drink it all in, to be at one with all the world before him and not be identified with any part of it. So he stood a pace or two apart from the hoppers, and watched with delight and wonder as the three boats rowed with a becoming majesty up to the starting post — each causing one group to jump and shout in frenzy — thinking that it should be given to such strength and beauty always to know victory. Then there was that moment ten minutes or so later when in spite of the uproar on the bank, the desperate shouts of encouragement, one crew alone swept on to victory, while the other two, the grace and majesty now gone, and fatigue, even weakness, appearing on their faces, slumped on their oars after crossing the finishing line. The crowd surged towards the boatsheds, where once again the boys from his school formed groups and began to hop, and sing, and shout the question, *"Who are we?"* and the reply, *"Grammar"*, just as the warmth began to go out of the day. And still he stood apart watching it all.

He was so carried away, both by the poetry and the majesty of the afternoon, that he joined a group for the long walk back to the school, and began to talk about the four flashes of foam on either side of the boats as the oars dipped, of the bows cutting the water and the colour in the water, the sky, the leaves with their autumn tints, and the city in the distance brooding untouched by all their sound and fury, until he noticed one boy nudge another and little giggles of derision pass from boy to boy. One boy said, "Our ickle man's a poet," and another added sarcastically, "But doesn't he half know it?" So he held his tongue for the rest of the long walk home, though, in his pain and confusion, he wanted to tell them, he used to say years later, that that was the whole point — he never could be a poet because he never could find the words to describe what was inside him. He felt that that was just another one of those unfair things in life — being born with such sensibilities, such awareness, but not with the verbal gifts to do anything about it. He was like somebody lost in a great fog, convinced that there was a way out to the light, and at times he lashed out at those who did him great evil as every now and then he rushed towards that light.

But on that day he was too carried away by the experience to entertain any dark thoughts about life or other human beings. He was looking forward to the treat the Housemaster had promised for them if Grammar won — a visit to the theatre to see "Good News". After the meal, which ended with the singing of the boarders' song:

> *You ought to be a boarder,*
> *For a week or two;*
> *You work all day,*
> *You get no pay,*
> *You're fed on Irish stew.*
> *The potatoes they are rotten*
> *And the meat it walks to you —*
> *You ought to be a boarder*
> *For a week or two!*

for a few moments everyone was so caught up in the gaiety of the moment, that boys looked at each other tenderly. It was a time for moistness in the eyes, and a reaching out for each other; and then away, the rush down the stairs, the agile and the daring taking four or even six at a time, the timid, the cautious and the clumsy not daring more than one. All were so caught up in the laughing, heaving pack that no frowns, no cries of "I'll get you for that!" countered the mood of the moment. With a shout of *"Grammar, Grammar, Ra, Ra, Ra,"* they were away, and on to the tram where, for the sake of decorum, they became suddenly stilled.

Then they climbed on to the cable tram in Bourke Street, where the movement up and down excited them again; and then there was the mad rush to the theatre, and climbing the never-ending flight of stairs, rounding each corner with hope followed by the low moan as they saw yet another flight, till, at last, at the very top, they filed into the "gods" for a seat in the front row, from where they could see deep below pearl-necklace-wearing women laughing at everything their male partners said. Charles wanted then one day to be as comfortable and witty as one of them. Then the light went out, and the magic began.

Up went the curtain, and while the orchestra played gaily, the drummer especially catching his eye for the frenzied way he fiddled with his sticks, suddenly young men and girls appeared dressed in holiday clothes, the men wearing straw boaters and the girls straw hats, with lovely fetching ribbons streaming from them as they moved, all of them swaying rhythmically to the music, till they reached the footlights where they sang gaily,

> *Good news is welcome to me,*

then glumly,

> *Bad news is hell come truly —*

a mood which only lasted an instant, and was gone like thistle-down before the winds of their gaiety, for that other theme came back, heralded by a gay trill on the cornet and a roll on the drums. They sang loudly,

> *Oh Mister good news,*
> *That's what I'm waiting for,*
> *GOOD NEWS.*

Then they all ran off the stage laughing and four men strolled on and sat down at a table and began to play cards, and behind one man, the most handsome of them all, who had a light in his eyes, and looked as though he could excel at everything, there was a most beautiful girl who seemed to want this young godling to win — to want that most desperately, and possibly to want other things as well which Charles did not understand as he was but thirteen at the time, and still innocent of those other hungers, and that war, and all the joy and all the humiliation in those deeds of darkness, and only saw then that for some inexplicable reason the young girl could not take her eyes off the man, and seemed to want him to succeed in everything. Every time he won she clapped her hands for joy till he, standing up, faced her, but instead of his looking happy a great darkness seemed to descend on him, as he said to her, holding her two hands in his, "You know — lucky in cards, unlucky in love." The mood of sadness seemed to overwhelm the other three players as well because they had no further stomach for the game, and tiptoed reverently off the stage just as the man, the godling, said, "What else matters if you're lucky in love?" — a question which made the girl turn thoughtful too. Her gay mood vanished, and while she looked serious, but still very lovely, the man began to sing:

> I don't mind if at poker I'm green,
> If I'm satisfied with a beautiful queen
> I'll say I'm lucky in love.
> Lucky in love,
> What else matters if you're lucky in love?

Many things happened after that, but it all ended happily, with the godling lucky in cards as well as in love, marrying the lovely girl and everyone singing again:

> Good news is welcome to me,
> Bad news is hell come truly.

By then the magic had gone out of the evening for Charles; or, rather, that chance remark by the man who looked as though all human achievements were open to him, that a man could be lucky at cards but unlucky in love — a remark the rest of the evening simply threw away — had started up something in his mind, something which had never occurred to him before. Without taking thought he had assumed that the words meant what they said — that unto him that hath, it shall be given — but here, suddenly in the midst of the excitements of the evening, the gaiety, the fun, the jokes, the laughing, and the music, where life was held up as one long round of pleasure, a beautiful young man had dropped the remark that you could be lucky or successful in some things, but not in others; say, love.

The chill of it swept over him, engulfing him, so that once again he wanted to be alone, to brood over what the man had said, and puzzle it out. So, after the play, he waited till all the others had jumped on the tram, and then hopped on the other end so that he could worry over the mystery of it — wondering whether this meant that if a man strove after some excellence, tried, say, to perfect himself as a pianist, a violinist, a mathematician, a physicist, or a historian, that he might not be lucky in love. Anyhow, what was luck? Was your luck your desert? Was what happened to you what ought to happen? Or was it all blind chance, just luck like playing cards? And if it was all luck, all blind chance, what was the point of trying, what was the point of effort? And why was it that the other boys did not seem to be interested in such questions? If there were questions, the answers to which affected all that happened to them in life, why were they not interested? Did this mean they did not care? If so, were there any other people who cared?

He began to wonder whether any of the masters cared. He could not believe the assistant chaplain cared, because the only time he had ever seen him look excited about anything was when he made that whinnying noise when he took out new tennis balls. Perhaps the headmaster cared, because there had been that wonderful moment, that never-to-be-forgotten moment that night late in April when he had come out into the quadrangle and rested his hand on the lamp-post — and indeed seemed to need to rest it there, as he was swaying slightly before he did so — and four or five boys, of whom Charles was one, looked up in awe and wonder out of the pool of darkness at his face, framed there against the great dome of the sky, and heard him say in a voice which seemed to express all the beauty, the horror and the mystery, wretchedness, despair and loneliness of life —"I went hunting, boys. . . . I can only hope one day you will all find life as beautiful as I did today."

What had he meant by that? Had he meant that the moments of beauty and happiness would be very few? Why did he, Charles, feel so drawn towards him? Did he, the headmaster, care about the things that were worrying Charles? The only time Charles had tried to say anything to him, they had not got very far. That was the time the headmaster had asked him, "Are you getting things straight?" And Charles had said, not cheekily, or showing off (because the headmaster conferred a dignity on others to which they themselves were often complete strangers) but shyly, and very tentatively, "Sometimes I wonder, sir, whether things ever do become straight." To which he had replied with sympathy, "Try hard and they will." But he did not try to persuade Charles that the crooked ever did become straight. Charles knew from listening to those lessons in the chapel on Sundays that whoever had written those ancient books had had the same doubts — "There is one event unto all." Sometimes in school they came on a line in poetry which spoke about this subject of his, which the master rushed over, and the other boys ignored. So, perhaps, on this, he would travel alone through life, just as then on the tram he travelled alone, haunted by those words: "Lucky in love . . . what else matters if you're lucky in love?"

It was as though he felt the need of some protection, something to stand between him and what other people menaced him with. It was in this mood of foreboding disaster, and the panic of seeing that he knew of nothing, either in himself, or outside himself, to prevent such disaster, that he went through all the routine of going to bed. He cleaned his teeth — but what good could cleanliness do to still those fears of what *they* might do to him? — and put on his pyjamas and knelt beside the bed, like all the other boys in the dormitory, and prayed while the prefect waited with his hand on the light switch. What good would that do him, was it likely that that mysterious One, who had made the world, but so far as mankind was concerned, had not been heard of since, would rescue him from *them*? Besides even if He rescued small boys from their tormentors, what had he, Charles, done to deserve such favours? And if the mysterious One either could not, or would not stir on his behalf, perhaps He might give him the strength to face his tormentors, and in his panic, he clutched at the promise that He would not suffer a man to endure more than he could bear. Besides, *they* were not to know that, and anyhow the prefect would soon stop that, because he must surely want to get down to his special supper room; and there — he knew it — were the words: "Hurry up! I can't spend all night while chaps like you say your prayers" . . . and off went the light . . . and with the darkness came the reminder, "No more talking, or I'll belt the hides off you."

There he lay, waiting for *them* to call, and when the door opened, he was so certain it would be for him that he was half out of bed when the face came out of the darkness, and the voice, "You're wanted in the Long Dorm," pausing just long enough to see the terror and hold his ear and say, "What are you so scared about? Anyone would think you were going to be murdered" . . . and laugh in his face. . . . And he followed him down the long corridor, between the rows of beds — the frightened eyes of the others turning in relief when they knew that *they* had got Charles for the night — till the closed door, on which he knocked, and heard the question: "Who's there?" and replied, "Hogan . . . Charles Hogan."

The door opened and a boy, much older than he, and taller, much taller, taunted him: "Why don't you want Grammar to win?" To which he replied, "But I do want Grammar to win." And one of *them* said, "If you want Grammar to win, why don't you barrack with the others?" to which he replied, "I couldn't help it." And one of *them* then said, "We are going to teach you to barrack . . . Climb on the piss-pot! And put your toes over the edge, and say as though you meant it, 'Come on, Grammar!'" Which he did, while *they* struck his toes, and beat his back and flicked at his face with knotted towels, and shouted: "Louder, louder, louder . . . barrack as though you meant it."

Not knowing how to pretend to such enthusiasm, not out of pride of obstinacy, because he was prepared to stoop to anything to get out of the flick of towel and tongue, but not having the power to do what his tormentors demanded, he tried desperately for that tone he knew *they* wanted, but could not find it, until, moment of panic, his voice seemed to get weaker just as they shouted all the more insistently: "Come on, louder, louder," until one boy, *their* leader, possibly out of tedium, said that was enough for one night, and they would go on with the lesson next sports night — "Let's finish off with unders and overs." So off he went, like a hunted animal, under one bed and over another, while *they* thrashed him with towels wetted and rolled into a kangaroo's tail — under and over the whole twelve beds, and then down the middle, and out again into that long corridor, between the beds, while the boys stared, but took no action, not whispering or murmuring sympathy, or asking whether they could help or do anything, not because they believed Charles had only got what he deserved, that *they* were doing that which they, the younger ones, secretly longed to do, but lacked the power; not from lack of sympathy with any victim of cruelty or bullying, but just out of self-protection.

Because that was what Charles had to face up to . . . that there was no one to turn to . . . that the boys who had seen were afraid to do anything . . . that he could not tell those who had not seen, because they would humiliate him . . . it would shame him to do so . . . and he could not speak to the masters because you did not do that sort of thing . . . or not in those cases, and although they were told there were some cases where you should speak to the masters and would not be classed as a squealer, he, Charles, had never found such a case. Perhaps he could tell it to the headmaster.

Perhaps, next time the headmaster asked him whether he was getting things straight, he could say there were some things which were not coming straight for him. But when he tried, he found the headmaster only exhorted him to "get his declensions and conjugations straight," and then those other things at which Charles had barely hinted would fall into place. He wondered about the assistant chaplain again . . . and all those promising words he recited every Sunday, which seemed to suggest that there was an issue out of all our afflictions; but whenever Hogan saw the chaplain his mind seemed to be on quite different things . . . and so again the words that came up from inside him, the anguish and the questions, returned to the place whence they came, unanswered.

One Sunday night soon after the towel bashing, he noticed

a shaft of light across the flagstones outside the main door of the chapel, and peered in. . . . Someone was playing the organ. Not daring to go in, he stood in the darkness with his back to the door, lost in wonder, because, as he listened, it seemed that the music was saying very much what he felt. As he listened there, sensing some mystery, he found some words to make it intelligible at least in part . . . that maybe there was no answer either to our moments of suffering or our moments of joy . . . that maybe, once you accepted that, once you no longer looked for justice or desert or reward, you saw some things were from eternity and would never change. The music seemed to promise an end to that sense of being alone, a grain of sand on an unending beach — an end to the terror of those never-ending blows . . . an end to the impotence, and a promise of completeness. And even if there was no one he could tell this to, some sort of peace had begun to settle deep inside him and, with it, the end of that desperate need that someone must come to his aid, or it would be too unfair . . . that hatred of others, because they left him to a fate he was impotent to evade. And he walked out of the darkness into the shaft of light. What did it matter if there was so little light for a man to stand in?

Learning to Bowl an Out-swinger

EVEN though there was not much light in which a man could stand, there were some fleeting moments for Charles Hogan when he was a boy at Belgrave, when the light shone clearly. There was that moment after breakfast one Sunday morning in the spring of 1930 — the year he turned fifteen. Bella, the maid, had just cleared the table and placed the ash-tray next to his father's breakfast cup. Sensing some glow of pride in the vicar, as even the simplest of women do, and knowing, as women do, just how much he loved to dwell on even the least of his achievements, she asked him, taking care he did not see her wink at Charles:

"What was the plate like this morning, vicar?"

"Phenomenal, Bella, absolutely phenomenal. I tell you, there hasn't been a collection like it for an early morning service since they first built churches in the mountain district."

"It just goes to show what a little human sympathy and understanding can do. Another cup of tea, vicar? A little early in the day for 'cold tea'?"

"Bella, there is a time for tea, and a time for 'cold tea'. Sunday, Bella, is a time for 'tea' — a fact, Bella, which makes it difficult to understand why the Lord blessed the seventh day and hallowed it."

The vicar lit a cigarette and drew in the smoke with as much pleasure as he enjoyed his joke. Soon, to the thud of the rolling pin on the white bread which Bella was preparing for the communion service at eleven, he began to speak again:

"Bound to be quiet at eleven, boy, after the great roll-up at eight. You can't expect them to turn up every time. And talking about record, did I ever tell you about the time I ate two dozen eggs for breakfast? Two dozen, did you hear what I said, boy? It was when the hospital ship, the *Karoola*, called at Ceylon. You remember, boy, when I was a stretcher-bearer in the A.I.F. Mind you, boy, we had had quite a bit of 'sarsaparilla' before we left the ship. I tell you, boy, the man who discovered sarsaparilla was a true friend of humanity. You can mix any drink you like with sarsaparilla and no one need be any the wiser — provided, boy, you remember my motto: 'Moderation in all things'. But take my tip, boy, never talk to women about sarsaparilla. They don't understand that sort of thing, boy."

Just as Charles was wondering whether he should risk to ask why women were the great nay-sayers, his father started up again:

"Do you remember the story, boy, about Jacob and his ladder? Now, you're a clever customer — you tell me why Jacob saw angels not just running up the ladder, to have a look at the people in heaven, but also saw them running down the ladder. Now, go on, boy, see if you can tell me why they are running down the ladder. Go on boy, don't be afraid to use your imagination."

"Do you think, perhaps, they wanted to take back to earth the glad tidings of what they had seen? Aren't angels God's messengers?"

"Quite right, boy, quite right. I'm as sure of it as I am of anything — as sure of it as I am that I'm sitting here. But, I'll let you into a secret, boy. Sometimes I think those descending angels are rushing down the ladder to warn us that the rulers of this world are also in charge in the next. Bishops, boy, priests, and bank managers — all those Pharisees and Philistines who nailed Christ to the tree — if you know what I mean, boy — the spiritual bullies of mankind have captured the kingdom of heaven. I can only hope, boy, there are gallons and gallons of 'cold tea' in Heaven, because if those angels are right we'll need our comforter there, too."

Just as Charles was quailing at the idea that the judge of the quick and the dead might have the face and values of his house-master, his father bounced off on to another subject. How was Charles to know then what three ports on an empty stomach did to a man's imagination?

"If you listen to the music of Bach, boy, you'd never believe Christ hung and suffered on that tree to help the spiritual bullies capture the kingdom of heaven. Do you remember that passage in St Matthew's Passion when Christ has just told the disciples He would break bread and drink of the fruit of the vine with them in Jerusalem, and they ask Him prosaically 'Where?' But then, boy, suddenly Bach shows us the majesty in the moment. Listen to the transition, boy [going to the piano]. This is the first 'Where'. Now listen carefully, boy, to the moment when reality is transcended — just a simple arpeggio in E minor by the strings, and we are lifted into another world, as Christ promised we would all one day be lifted up. Listen to that second 'Where', boy. Do you hear what it is saying: even if the Christ-like are not in charge here, there will be a time when we shall understand why people like us are tormented here — a time, boy, when that torment will cease — I'm sure of it, boy — sure as I am of anything. And that's what Bach tells us, boy, in the last great chorus of the St Matthew Passion, to accept it all, because one day the great agony is going to end. Listen to this great hymn of acceptance, boy — listen to how the music both teaches us what it is we have to accept, and gives us the strength to accept it. Listen, boy." And he began to sing, his eyes moist and shining, "In tears of grief, dear Lord, we leave thee," just as Charles's mother opened the door, and asked:

"Who's going to ring the first bell for the eleven o'clock service?"

"Did you ever know the bell not to be rung on time?"

"The way you two carry on the parishioners would think you must be mental."

"Look, I tell you again, my dearest, the bell will be rung in time. Did you hear what I said? The bell will be rung on time. I will so do, the Lord being my helper."

Then the mother closed the door quietly, muttering to herself that "no living person would stand it". Charles, who always felt fright and dismay when people he loved needled each other, just wanted her to leave the room quickly, because then he would be released from his terror that a further pester from his mother would provoke some desperate act by his father, some cruel, mocking remark which would start her crying again.

Happily, with the passage of time man and wife had learnt that the painful consequences of retaliation far exceeded the immediate satisfactions, and had come to avoid head-on collisions which led to savage exchanges of resentments. The Reverend Mr Hogan had given up much in life — even his great rages. It was perhaps significant that fond though he was of quoting the words of the Saviour, the one remark he avoided like the plague was that one that whoever was angry without cause would be in danger of the judgment. This time he just waited till she had gone, and swivelled round on the piano stool, a tiny gesture salvaged from the wreck of his great rages, and said to Charles:

"Do you remember this passage from Stainer's 'Crucifixion', boy?" He struck a tremulous chord, decorating it with his usual rumbles in the left hand, and said:

"Listen to me, boy," as he sang "Is it nothing to you all ye that pass by?" Then, as though disgusted with himself for this indulgence in self-pity, perhaps resenting too the other fate of not being able to tell his boy, who seemed to understand so much, that he had reached that stage in life where he had a great hunger for love but could neither love nor be loved, and wanting so much to tell him that that was what he would like to sing about, if only God had given him the capacity to match his desire — which was the great pain of his life: that eternal sense of inadequate powers — he lapsed into tomfoolery on the piano, using as ever buffoonery to ease his pain and purge his own sentimentality and self-pity. He ended with a feverish run up the scale to a quite hysterical high G, followed by a resolved chord . . . after which he gently let down the lid of the piano, just as Charles asked whether it would help if he rang the first bell. To which his father agreed, adding "Anything for a quiet home." It was as though he could not allow the simplest moments to pass without offering some general comment on life, and then despise himself for the triviality or banality of the comment.

As Charles Hogan tolled the bell, he could see his father walk briskly towards the vestry door, holding the chalice in one hand, and using the other hand to balance the paten which contained Bella's cubes of bread, enclosed in a snow-white cloth. Charles could see the pleasure on the faces of the parishioners as his father passed. He saw his father rejoice with those that were rejoicing, and mourn with those that were sad. He saw how he pressed the arms of all of them. Charles wondered whether perhaps this made it appropriate for his father to ask those in the congregation who were in love and charity with their neighbour, and intended to lead a new life, to draw near with faith and take that holy sacrament to their comfort meekly kneeling upon their knees. If this were so, why was it that his mother, who never allowed herself the liberties as a condemner so wantonly indulged in by his father (who was fond of quoting St Paul's text for the savagers of mankind: "Alexander the coppersmith did me great evil. The Lord reward him according to his works") — why was it that she who seldom wore a frown when her neighbours behaved in a way which was displeasing to her, was rarely at ease with other people, nor were they often at ease with her? Why was it that she who only wanted to do the will of her Father in Heaven never knew what it was like to bathe in the warm sunlight of human regard? What was the source of her never-ending pain, her everlasting misery? Was this what the wise men of old meant when they talked of "woman's sadness"? Why was it that she always seemed to stand as the eternal judge of what he wanted to do. Why was it that if he ever dared to speak to her about these things, he became aware of some vileness in himself? Was that why he felt a bond with his father — the bond between men who bore a guilty stain like the mark of Cain?

Why, for example, had his mother let drop her wish that he would not waste his time talking to Mr Buscombe, just when he was beginning to enjoy talking to him? Everything about the man was extravagant — the huge shock of white hair, the outsize cravat kept in place by a pearl-topped pin, and a language to match his appearance. Besides, there was about him a suggestion that he knew something which had eluded Charles Hogan and his family, a hint that he knew something they did not know despite all their striving, their strutting, and their fretting. Every Sunday morning Charles used to watch Mr Buscombe walking briskly towards the Austral Hall for mass, looking like a man who knew where he could eat the bread of eternal life. Yet, just as he began to feel a great tug towards Buscombe, his mother had planted those seeds of doubt in his mind, not by absolute prohibition, but by making him feel he was peculiar to want to speak to Buscombe. And when he had pressed her to say why, all she had allowed herself to say was that it was both peculiar and queer.

So he had had to make quite sure his mother was not looking when he met Buscombe, because going without Buscombe, sacrificing him out of loyalty to his mother's desires, was something which had never occurred to him. Betrayal had not been a conscious choice, but rather a subterfuge to enable him to continue his discovery of the world of men. It was the same with Bill Pitcher, one of the local garagemen, who had told him that the Russian revolution would remove all the dirt from human life, and give men a new confidence in their powers, and stop all this Christian grovelling about unworthiness, and being washed clean in the blood of the Lamb. "Mind you, Charles," he had added, your mother won't be too keen on her own boy consorting with her adversary, the Devil. She'll tell you to resist me, steadfast in the faith." The disappointing thing had been that his mother had gone further and had advised him to stay away. When he had pressed her to give a good reason, again she had warned him people would think he was peculiar if he enjoyed speaking to a Bolshevik.

He had always wanted to have his hair cut by Lal Friend.

Every Saturday morning on the rear window of a Buick sedan parked outside his shop, Lal had chalked "To Ferntree Gully And Return. Five Bob. Driver guaranteed sober." Charles loved to buy his father's cigaretes from Lal because in the brief time he was in the shop he could hear from behind the curtain which separated the shop from the billiard saloon, the clicking of billiard balls, the clink of glasses, and snatches of conversation about what one man was planning to do to Kitty Malone after the picture show on Saturday night, or what another man would do to "that animal from the Gully" next time they met on the football field, followed by much belly laughter. But when he had risked telling his mother about their gaiety, taking care to suppress the subject of their wit, his mother had not dismissed it as the laughter of fools like unto the thorns crackling under a pot, but had dropped the mysterious remark that she hoped her boy would not grow up fascinated by low life, and asked him to promise that in future he would always allow Mr Bradley to cut his hair. Which he had done, only to find to his everlasting regret that old Bradley only had two topics of conversation — both gloomy. One was to place his hand like a bishop about to confirm a boy over Charles's hair, and say, not "Bless this child," but rather, "You won't be keeping this for long." To which Charles wanted to say that if God had to number the hairs of many people with hair as thick as Bradley's, He would be spending His time adding up instead of judging. Bradley's other conversation move was to say, while at the rear of Charles, that from what he could hear of what went on in the other barber's shop on Saturday nights, Belgrave was going to the dogs. When Charles remained silent, Bradley would walk solemnly round to the front of the chair, and look so fiercely into his eyes, snipping away with the scissors at some imaginary evil which needed excision, that Charles had felt he had no alternative but to drop his eyes from that cruel gaze and murmur a weak assent, and hope not to reproach himself harshly because he had even lacked the courage to let a man like Bradley know the secrets of his heart.

Then there had been all those part-comic, part-painful scenes brought on by his mother's insistence on saying to all and sundry, "There's one thing I will say for my boy, Charles. He's got brains." It was not so much the imputation that he had little if anything else — though heaven knows that was bad enough, seeing how his mother had planted that seed in his mind about being peculiar. It was rather what Charles had to pay for his mother's pride. The reputation for cleverness had led to an invitation to listen to Vern McIlwraith's new short-wave wireless. "Your brother," Vern had explained, "can have a dance with the wife in the parlour while we tune-in London." So he had had to sit there in Vern's den pretending to understand such words as super-heterodyne, direct-coupling, push-pull, and electrolytic condensers, while his brother danced with Vern's wife, a "pretty little thing," as his mother put it, who, in between the "joeys" and static coming from Vern's loud-speaker, whispered to him gaily, "It must be wonderful to be so brainy"; and then had proceeded, while her husband was not looking, to carry out literally the advice in the song to which they were dancing:

And I seem to find the happiness I seek,
When we're out together dancing cheek to cheek.

When he and his brother had walked home together his brother had said that when they arrived they would have a really good talk together as he had something to tell him. But when they had reached home, and undressed and put on pyjamas, and said their prayers, his brother, when at long last he got into bed after his lengthy petitions or words of gratitude to the deity, said it would have to be another night because he was just too dog-tired to keep his eyes open. Then he had got out of bed and had said he wanted to pray again, which had made Charles wonder whether it had anything to do with dancing with Mrs McIlwraith, because talking about wireless circuits had not planted any desire in him for further communion with the deity. His brother rose suddenly and had said another mysterious thing: he had said he "felt better"; adding, "You've no idea how tired I am." Then he had added through a yawn that if they were to get a good possie in the outer at Carlton next day they would need to get there well before two, because a game between Carlton and Geelong was always very "crowd-pleasing". Then he had fallen sound asleep, while Charles had lain there wondering what it must be like to be

53

friendly both with a woman and with God.

Then there had been the family row about whether there should be dancing after the whist and euchre drive to raise funds for the church. Charles and his brother had wanted dancing after the euchre, though they had hesitated to tell their mother why. But she had been dead set against it, and when they had asked her what was wrong with dancing, she had said she did not think God's work should be financed by pandering to the baser passions of mankind. The Reverend Hogan had replied that it took all sorts to make a world. He knew that the appearance of Kitty Malone and her "button-on" style of dancing, which seemed to give the men so much pleasure, would help to boost the vicar's holiday fund. A long run of wet Sundays in July and August had been such a thin time for plates that he wondered whether perhaps he would have any help at all with his "cold tea" during his annual fishing trip to Phillip Island. The Reverend Hogan, always a man to believe that God moved in a mysterious way his wonders to perform, had settled the argument by saying that he would ask the vestry and see what they thought, knowing quite well he could twist them round his little finger. When "cold tea" supplies were endangered by the moral scruples of his wife, he had perfected the cunning of the serpent.

His mother had accepted the vestry's decision with a good grace, but had taken the boys into her room and made them promise on their honour that they would not ask Kitty Malone for a dance, a promise Charles, for his part, had given with some guile because he knew what his mother did not know — that in all the sets, the Alberts, the Fitzroys and the Lancers, and in the progressive barn-dance, with any luck and some skill a man could do quite well for himself with all the pretty girls on the floor. What he called his "accidentally-done-on-purpose" technique. He was becoming his father's boy. Besides, it had amused him to imagine how any man could do any good for himself with Kitty at a local dance so long as her father and brother stood guard over the one exit door in the Soldiers Memorial Hall with zeal equal to the guards of the Vestal Virgins in Roman times.

As usual the vestrymen and members of the ladies' guild had

taken precautions lest the music should heighten desire and lessen control. Art Chandler would be playing the fiddle gaily but not suggestively. There would be no saxophone, that instrument which was calculated to weaken a woman's power to say "no", and strengthen, alas, to an alarming degree, a man's expectation of "yes". Florrie Chandler would play the piano. She was a good strummer, Florrie, a good sort who liked to see young folk enjoy themselves, but not a one to play those seductive American tunes with words which might put ideas into the heads of the unwary, especially if Kitty Malone's skirt swirled up above her knees just as someone crooned the words, "The longer that you linger in Virginia the more you long to stay."

Towards the end of the euchre Kitty Malone had come in, with a cape over her shoulders which the matrons of Belgrave had accepted as a temporary reprieve, while the young men were prepared to wait for the music to start, because then they would be able to see all they were expected to be able to see — at least on the dance floor. Art Chandler had begun to run the bow over the strings, while his wife struck A loudly. Charles Hogan and his brother had cut thin strips off candles, and the young boys and girls had enjoyed themselves skidding along the floor-boards till they had become so slippery that Art Chandler had said if they put any more on the dancers would come one hell of a cropper.

Then the music had started. Art and Florrie had played a few bright bars of a well known quickstep, and then stopped while Newt McLardy, the local grocer, with a face as red as a beetroot, and a voice like a rasp, Hogan's father used to say, but underneath a heard of gold and a prince of good fellows, had called out:

"And now, ladies and gentlemen, take your partners for the Alberts please."

Charles had asked Mrs Newt McLardy to be his partner, because, though somewhat ungainly, and much lighter on her own feet than on his, she was a bit of a sport, who fluttered her arms like a bird in the waltz parts of the Alberts, and had a light in her eye that suggested perhaps an awareness of or even a hankering after better things than just weighing out pounds of sugar in Newt McLardy's grocer's store. So he had bowed before her, and she had looked quite pleased, and had said he should be dancing with someone of his own age. And he had said that what she lacked in beauty she more than made up for by her air of distinction — a remark which had caused a glow to pass over her face and spread down to her shoulders, just as Charles had seen that the pair opposite them in the set was Kitty Malone and Colin Carrington. That in turn had made him glow so much that Mrs McLarty had said, "I have to admit she's pretty."

These were not the words Charles Hogan would have used to describe Kitty. To look at her in profile she resembled a woman on whom nature had practised a cruel joke. The front teeth were so prominent that she was not able to close her mouth. This left her with a suggestion of expectancy, an impression strengthened by what she had done to herself with rather rough use of the curling tongs and crude dye on thinning wiry hair. So what with the rouge dabbed on roughly on both cheeks, and a habit of chewing gum incessantly, and humming a tune, as though to soothe some private sorrow or uproar of her own, she put Charles at a loss to explain why she drew men unto her. Years later he would have had no difficulty: she was a loin-stirrer on a grand scale. All he was aware of then was of a light dancing in her eyes. Then Newt McLardy had shouted above the music, "Ladies and gentlemen, bow to partners." Charles had bowed with an exaggerated flourish to Mrs McLardy who as she raised her head whispered that she could not see what the men saw in Kitty, that her Newt was as silly as a coot every time Kitty came into the shop. Then Newt McLardy had called out:

"Ah — now, ladies and gentlemen, if you please, first lady and hopposite gent, hadvance into centre, swing, and waltz to places."

This meant that Hogan had to take Kitty's two hands in his, point his left foot towards hers and propel her by using his right foot like a pedal; which he did, leaning back the while, until the tip of his shoe, the tip of her shoe, the swirling skirt, the music and the pleasure on Kitty's face the faster he moved, seemed to blend into something more. It was as though they too had been lifted up, and were becoming like gods. Charles wanted it to go on and on, but soon the tempo of the music had changed into the steady three-four time of the waltz, which had caused them both to prop, to sway, to see the room and all the people in the room move drunkenly, till Kitty had held out her arms towards him as she had buttoned on down below, and had pressed her bosom gently against his breast. Then he had almost let out a cry of pleasure, as though he were now close to knowing what other men knew about Kitty, but women never knew.

"You're different from the others," she had said.

He had wanted to say so many things to her, only all the words that had come into his mind were other people's words. He had believed her worthy of something to match the music, the dancing, and the magic of her body, but he had only managed to say:

"You're as light as a feather."

Then the music had stopped and he had to go back to Mrs McLardy, and look pleased and find something to say when she had asked him wasn't she a bit like a sack of potatoes after Kitty; adding, "I have to admit she does dance beautifully." What was worse, he had to keep his solemn promise to his mother that under no circumstances would he ask Kitty Malone for a dance. So once again a commandment from his mother — her "Thou shalt not dance with Kitty Malone," making eleven commandments all told — had reminded him of Jehovah. Both of them were always coming between him and what he wanted to do.

After the routine assurance from his brother that one day they simply must have a really long talk, only not that night, as he was simply fagged out, he had climbed into his bed. He had rushed through the Our Father during which, although he had tried to put some fervour in the words "Thy kingdom come . . ." it had seemed quite clear that what he had really wanted was that Kitty should come to him immediately. But the only person who had come to him that night had been his mother, who, hearing the commotion from her ever restless son, had appeared to him in the dark, and had told him, seeing how nervy he had been all night, she had decided to send him to have a long talk with Dr Tory, and how she had prayed that night to her Father in Heaven that "morally, Charles, dear, everything was all right". And, after she had kissed him goodnight once again, he had lain there wondering why he had to see a doctor, because Kitty had opened up a new world to him. Surely no one would want to take that from him.

The talk with Dr Tory was a bit of a joke. Old Tory, as he and his brother called him, was one of those failures in life who spend all their time telling others the fruits of their wisdom. He was a vain, pompous ass who, long after he had become a standing joke amongst his fellow specialists in Collins Street, thought his words might be heeded in the mountain district. He had begun by asking Charles whether he knew how to bowl an out-swinger with a cricket-ball. When Charles, too proud to say no, had stood silent, he had taken a tennis ball, and had shown him how, if you placed the thumb under the ball, splayed the second and third fingers on top of the ball and threw it into the wind, the ball would go straight for ten to fifteen yards, and then curve sharply from right to left. That was called an out-swinger. Then looking so deep into Charles's eyes that the latter had dropped his to the ground, he had added that Charles had realized already that a new curve was starting in his life. As his mother had just reminded him, Charles was the brainy member of the family. That, by the way, was all the more reason for caution. Thinking never taught a man how to live. Remember the words of the Saviour — "Which of you by taking thought, can add a cubit to his stature?" — wonderful chap — a man who had the heart of the matter in him — a man, my dear Charles, who moved cleanly through life, no curves, or out-swingers on his life, ha, ha, ha. Then old Tory had put in his parting shot — "Try it out in the nets when you get back to school, and don't forget who taught you how to bowl an out-swinger when you skittle their stumps."

As soon as cricket started that spring of 1930, soon after the grand-final of the footy and show-day, he had gone to the under-sixteen net which was being looked after by the assistant chaplain . . . who, dressed in his Oxford College cap, flannel shirt, cream trousers and buckskin boots, always seemed to

Charles to be a strange follower of that innocent one who had once walked beside the waters of Galilee plucking the ears of corn. Ignoring the assistant chaplain's banter that he knew Hogan had some claims to be considered a batsman, but as a bowler he was like his hand-writing — quite incomprehensible, untidy, and all over the place — he had taken the ball, measured out a run (despite more chaff from the assistant chaplain) and bowled. Sure enough, the ball had behaved just as Dr Tory had said it would. It had moved straight down the line of the leg stump for fifteen yards, then, just before it had pitched on the turf, it had dipped so sharply towards the off stump that the batsman had been baffled, had missed it, and the ball had knocked the off stump out of the ground, just as Hogan had turned to the assistant chaplain for a sign of recognition.

"Very good, Hogan, very good. Our ickle poet has become quite a bowler."

"Still got a lot to learn, sir."

"We all have a lot to learn, Hogan. You're like Martha, Hogan. One thing is missing."

"What's that, sir?"

"Pace off the pitch, Hogan, pace off the pitch."

"And how do you learn that, sir?"

"You don't learn that, Hogan. You've either got it, or you haven't got it. You're born with it."

The other boys had laughed and laughed, that one of their number was not going to get what he wanted. Years later he liked to think that had been the time when he had suddenly remembered the words about how the hand of the potter had faltered. But he could not even get the words of a quotation straight, so how could he be expected to enter in at the narrow gate?

Portrait of a Freethinker

PEOPLE used to say Steve Parsons had two versions of the story about himself and the bishop. There was the authorized version which he used when there was only time for one round of drinks before closing time; there was the revised version which he used when there was time for three or four more rounds. He had been telling the story in the back bar of the Swanston Family every Friday evening for the last fifteen or twenty years.

On one Friday evening which Charles Hogan was to remember, there was barely time for the authorized version; the barman had already called for the first time "Time gentlemen, please", when Parsons broke into a small group of undergraduates and asked, "Did I ever tell you about the night I stopped being a knee-bender? I was explaining to the bishop why I had decided not to enter the church. When I told him I could have nothing to do with a god who condemned more than half the people he created to everlasting punishment, the bishop gave me a knee press under the table. 'Steve, my boy,' he bleated in his poofter's voice, 'unless we drink our Saviour's blood we shall all assuredly be damned. Let us say together the words our Lord himself has told us to use: Our Father . . .' Well, that was the last time I bent the knee. When I rose to my feet I decided to dedicate myself to the noblest cause of all, the liberation of mankind from the lies of religion!"

When he had finished speaking, one of the few undergraduates who were listening to him offered to buy him a drink. Parsons said to make his a double whisky and a beer chaser as time was running short. So Charles Hogan shyly ordered the drinks, and as he placed them next to Parsons on the bar, whispered to him that it was for the cause.

"Look here, Charles, my boy," Parsons said, "I would like to tell you that I find it enormously encouraging that a talented man like you should want to spend his time drinking with a derelict like me . . . a man who has suffered for dedicating the best years of his life to the cause of human progress."

As Hogan's response to his challenge was, to say the least, inadequate — Hogan could only manage to say haltingly, "We all know how you missed the final honours ex. in history twenty years ago because you were not prepared to stoop" — Parsons took over. "I've fought for twenty years against the life-deniers," he declaimed, "against all the parsons and priests who peddled the lie about original sin, who encouraged men to beat their breasts and call themselves miserable sinners rather than seek pleasure drinking the fruit of the vine, or taking exercise in the cot."

And again Parsons hinted he had the power to uncover some secret for the young, that he could take them on a journey during which much that puzzled them in life would be made plain. So when he suggested Hogan might like "to make good night a certainty" by risking a filet mignon at the Italian, washed down with some good Hunter River claret, with cigars, coffee royals and some conversation about a man's love-life to follow, Hogan felt that perhaps this was the beginning of a journey in which he might learn how to feel noble while doing what he always wanted to do.

By this time he had had just sufficient beer for another strange and wonderful thing to happen to him: all those silly, stupid, hateful faces which he had loathed when he had entered the bar were changing into people to whom he wanted to talk. This quickened his gratitude to Parsons for working this miracle, though try as he would he could not find the words in which to express his feeling.

Even after they moved from the bar out on to the street and walked with the crowd down Swanston Street all he could manage was to talk about something quite different:

"I would like to tell you something," he started, "er . . . something I could only say to a man like you."

"Go on, Charles, my boy, unload."

"I'm escaping from my upbringing. I'm trying not to be hunted by shame and guilt and fears of damnation."

"Charles, my boy, as they say in the medical advertisements in the *Age* every Saturday morning, 'Successful treatment of particularly obstinate cases is guaranteed'."

They both laughed, but, somewhat to Hogan's disappointment, this was the end rather than the beginning of talking about himself. Parsons had another subject:

"Those teachers of yours, Charles, my boy, who have prostituted their talents every year to ensure that every generation of students does not know why a few are very rich and the many very poor, do they leave you any time to read the men who have taught mankind how this can be changed?"

"Do you think I ought to read Marx, and Lenin, and Stalin? . . ."

"You'll find more wisdom in Lenin on imperialism, than in the works of Major Barnes on the same subject, my boy."

Again they laughed, and Parsons added: "It takes courage for a man to identify himself with the progressive forces in this country, where the name of every man of good will is in the files of the security service. But you won't find the names of many of your professors in that roll of honour."

"I think . . . you know, I think the heart of one of our lecturers is in the right place. He was deeply moved when he quoted Chif's speech about the light on the hill. Another time he told us the true men of good will in Australia were those who were inspired by Christ and 1917."

Then Parsons smiled as an elder person does when a younger

person has spoken like a child, and said,

"All bourgeois idealist nonsense of course. We must tear the mask of these bourgeois illusions off the minds of the young, though in the meantime we can use Joe Gwatkin to radicalize them. He's vain enough to believe he is tilling the soil for the future of humanity, though one day we will force him to face reality or stop talking, and I think he will choose to face reality, because good-will Joe would prefer his audience in the Public Lecture Theatre to the refresher courses on bourgeois illusions we propose to conduct at Alice Springs shortly after we take over. He will want to make a speech on the day we turn St Pat's into a museum for the anti-godlies, and convert Young and Jackson's into the Sharkey and Gibson Home of Rest and Culture!"

This made Hogan suddenly feel lost and lonely and rather frightened. They walked in silence till they reached Bourke Street where Parsons decided to hail a cab rather than walk the rest of the way because, as he put it, he was still feeling the strain of a hard war. Besides, the drive might freshen him up for the chat. Again Hogan felt hopeful, and said he would pay for the cab, and when Parsons demurred and said he would only let Hogan pay if Hogan insisted, Hogan said, "But I do insist . . . I . . . you see . . . Let me at least show this little appreciation for a man who has sacrificed himself for . . ." But he could not quite manage to add "the noblest cause of all". So Parsons helped him by saying quietly, "I think I know what you mean."

After they entered the cab they threw their heads back on to the seat, and laughed together till Parsons broke off his laughter and said with some of the sternness as well as some of the majesty of a secular prophet, "Remember, Charles my boy, it is the cause of the people, and they must prevail in the end."

Hogan wanted to say it might be *their* cause, but it was not his cause as yet, but he was afraid Parsons might not like that very much, or might even frown at any facetiousness on such a serious subject. So he decided to say nothing until he could think of something which would appeal to Parsons.

"You know, Steve," he said after a minute or two of silence, "Joe Gwatkin told a number of us the other day in the Caf that the confessional was the Vatican's method of controlling Australian foreign policy."

"Charles, my boy, they say you're scarcely inside the Department of External Affairs in Canberra before you hear the chink of the Rosary beads. Charles, my boy, those men have two ambitions in life: to drop the bomb on Moscow, and to make damn certain no man or woman in Australia ever enjoys a night in bed in his life. Those vermin want to cheat simple people of the one pleasure they can have in life for nothing. It takes years to tear out the cancer those vermin leave in the mind, and sometimes, Charles, my boy, we're too late . . . yes, too late."

As Parsons said this, Hogan noticed a catch in the voice, which surprised him because though he knew that underneath the ribaldry, the Rabelaisian gusto and language in which Parsons always discussed the priests and sex, Parsons was in fact seriously committed to his own point of view, he had never known Parsons to be troubled or ruffled or disturbed in the pursuit of those views. What had originally attracted him to Parsons was just this monumental certainty, this almost insolent confidence which enabled him to participate in any conversation without those painful hesitations, those fumblings for words, which characterized all his own performances when subjects on which he felt deeply came up for discussion. All he could manage by way of comfort for Parsons were a few words: "All believers in happiness . . . er . . . that is to say . . . all men of good will have always been maligned as enemies of the people. Didn't Christ have some angry words to say about the men who raised statues to the men their spiritual ancestors had destroyed?"

"Charles, my boy, how many times must I ask you to keep that man out of any conversation with me?"

When they entered the cafe at the top of Bourke Street the head waiter bowed deeply to Parsons: "Your usual table at the window is waiting for you, sir." But the table had to wait quite a while for Parsons, while he paused at each table on the way for a few ha-ha's with the men, and a confidential whisper to the women followed by a gentle squeeze of the elbow with the right hand and a look of insight, sympathy and understanding on his face. After they sat down Parsons continued to exchange silent greetings with the other diners, to some raising his eyebrows, to others just lifting the index finger slightly off the tablecloth, while to some he maintained a dumb, gestureless communion which fascinated Hogan.

When they settled down to their sherry and the generous plates of minestrone (Parsons had asked the waiter to make them *grandi* and told Hogan to excuse his lapsing into Italian with the waiter, because culture was his substitute for a tip) Parson's gestures and conversation became at once more authoritative and confidential. He swept the room with his eyes, and leaned towards Hogan in a manner which the latter knew was an invitation, if not a command, for him to lean towards Parsons:

"Leo's here . . . the sort of fellow you ought to cultivate . . . a foundation member of the Party, and over thirty years in the rationalist movement . . . I'd like to bring the two of you together . . . I've got Leo to thank for introducing me to Maureen . . . I see he's putting Lance Packard back on the rails. A talented writer, Lance, full of insights into the human situation . . . you might have read what I had to say about him in the last issue of *Meanjin*. . . . There are great creative talents in the Australian people, if only their minds could be liberated from the obscurantist, reactionary nonsense pumped into them by the priest, the parson and the newspapers." Parsons paused to swallow the remaining spoonfuls of the minestrone, mop up the plate with a few slices of Vienna loaf, wash it down with a tumbler of claret, and light up a cigarette for a few puffs while they were waiting for the arrival of the filet mignon.

"We've got to give the people a new confidence in themselves. . . . This Maureen, whom I met at a cottage evening a few years ago . . . I've told you about her" (as a matter of fact he hadn't, but Hogan was too entranced to interrupt the flow) ". . . the black crows had so frightened her her eyes never stopped moving once. I decided, Charles, my boy, to teach her she would find that peace of God which passeth all understanding between the sheets rather than on her knees. Remember, Charles, my boy, even the apostles were exceedingly sorrowful when they learned there was to be none of the slap and tickle on the resurrection morning."

"And did she like it?"

"Like it, my boy? . . . She was enraptured. . . . When she came to me she had been roused by her husband, but not satisfied. . . . He had been taught by the Brothers to get it over quick and then rid his mind of all impure thoughts before falling asleep by fixing his mind at the foot of the cross. It's in their catechism for such as are of riper years. . . . She lay in agony beside him while he fingered his way to heaven on his Rosary beads. Poor sod, the Brothers had taught him marriage was the giving of one body to another for the purpose of fornication. . . . These people besmirch everything they touch."

By then they had moved on to brandy and cigars. Parsons had become so engrossed in his subject that he stopped signalling to the other diners. His voice became tired; he was supporting his massive face with one hand, and tapping his cigar gently on the edge of the ashtray with the other hand. In such moods he was fond of telling the young it had been a tiring war. But tonight he chose to unburden himself about Maureen.

"I began to educate her too, Charles, my boy. . . . I enlightened her on the source of her husband's income from the rubber plantations in Malaya. . . . He was bumped off by the Japanese when the English were busy defending themselves down to the last Australian . . . I had been reading about the exploitation of man by man . . . I had introduced her to the role of religion in the class struggle . . . I gave her Palme Dutt to read on India, and Bertrand Russell on *Why I am not a Christian*. . . . I was about to lend her Joyce's *Ulysses* when she rang me up to say she thought we had better stop seeing each other. I wormed it out of her that she had been to confession . . . 'Help me Father,' I suppose she said, 'because I have sinned.' . . . The black crow refused to grant her absolution unless she promised not to see me alone again. . . . When he asked her whether she was sorry she had offended God, she asked him how could the glad feel sorry. So he had to put the fear of hell into her by asking whether she was sorry to endanger her eternal salvation. And when she said, 'Yes, Father, yes, I am,' the swine absolved her. . . . And he told her the next time she was tempted she should send up a petition to the Virgin for

66

a smile of encouragement. . . . What superstitious twaddle, Charles, my boy, about a woman whose bones have been fertilizing the soil near Jerusalem ever since the days of the emperor Tiberius, as every good student of history knows."

A look of triumph spread over Parsons's face, as though his struggle against the forces of darkness and superstition had conferred on him a majesty such as descends on a man who has fought heroically against the destructive forces in nature.

"I told her, Charles, my boy, she'd be waiting a long time for that smile, and while she was waiting she'd better fortify herself with a cup of coffee and cigarette in one of the basement cafes in Collins Street. . . . After the coffee we moved round to the Swanston Family for a few quiet drinks . . . where I told her she might as well stay in town for a filet mignon at the Italian rather than dine in solitary squalor in her bed-sitting in East Melbourne. I ordered my standard inflaming dinner at the Italian of oysters, ravioli, filet mignon and coffee royals and then took her to East Melbourne. . . . And there, Charles my boy, she experienced once again the peace of Parsons rather than the peace of God."

Parsons sipped his brandy: "But she was back in the box before breakfast next morning. . . . This time the black crow so frightened the lights out of her that she took the next plane to Sydney."

Parsons paused a moment before he added with a mocking sweep of the hand, "And so, Charles my boy, a soul was saved for Christ, but lost to humanity and the cause of human progress."

"How about a stirrup cup before we leave?"

"No thanks, Charles, my boy, hardened old reprobate that I am, I never allow the sun to rise on a new day without making quite sure the night before that my wife will wake up cowlike and contented."

And for the first time that night Hogan noticed that Parsons's shirt-cuffs were grubby.

"'Twere Best Not Know Myself"

I REMEMBER there was something about her face which first caused my mind to linger longer over her than over other callers at our house on the hillside just nineteen miles east of Melbourne. My wife used to call our house "Liberty Hall" because all the children on the hillside played there all day, and all those who did not travail but were still heavy laden gathered there every Friday night to ease their burdens.

So there was nothing odd in her making a request to my wife to use the telephone. What was odd was the abruptness and the directness — the absence of ceremony in someone who said in her second sentence, "As you can tell from my voice, I'm English, you know, but please don't hold that against me. I know how you Australians feel about Poms. I'm rather on your side in that," and giggled a little, and began to flick through the pages of the telephone book. "You don't mind if I smoke, do you? Beastly habit, but I don't seem to be able to do without them. Marion fetch Mummy an ashtray. Go on, stupid, the man won't kill you. . . . She misses her father. . . . They all do. . . .

Stop the fidgets, girl. Blast, it's one of those Australian clots who doesn't seem to understand the English language. I say, Mr Hogan — Irish, I presume. I adore the Irish when they are not Catholic — I say Mr Hogan, would you be an angel and get the number for me. . . . Thanks. . . . How sweet of you. I do so much enjoy being helped by a sensitive and intelligent man. . . .

"Oh, hello, yes, it's me, Kathleen. . . ." There was something in the tone of her voice which told me that she was talking to a lover. I got up to leave the room — a move which caused her to place her hand over the receiver, and say, "Now don't you be English, Mr Hogan. I'm only arranging for a music lesson. You know that, don't you, Marion darling?" So I went back to my Housman — that queer spiritual food for most "future of humanity" men in Melbourne at the end of the war. Marion stood very close to her mother, who stroked her hair gently while Kathleen finalized time and place for that music lesson.

I remember thinking at the time that, judging by the animated face, the bright light that seemed to be switched on behind her eyes when time and place were mentioned, that it was going to be more than exercises in scales and arpeggios. But when I said this later to my wife she replied, "Trust you to think of that. You always have the whole creation groaning or copulating" — a remark which ended that subject for the day between us. But not for me. I began to wonder why it was that a woman who had about her an air of slovenliness, what with wearing green felt slippers in the middle of the day, heels crushed beneath both feet, no stockings despite rivers of veins in her legs, and a flabbiness about her knees, could touch men at all. It was the face which caused me to linger on her half in pity, half in question. There was a puffiness beneath the eyes; there were creases round the mouth, which, paradoxically was very small for a woman who in all her other behaviour suggested the word "loud-mouthed". It looked smudged, as though it had been stained or even possibly dirtied by life. But perhaps that is the sort of thing one would like to believe one thought on first seeing her, and certainly well before finding out what life had done to her.

When she left I said to my wife, for whom, by the way, a

crease on a face and shadows under the eyes were not hints of damnation but wounds which could and should be bathed: "Well, what do you make of her?" She replied in that tone she always used when she wanted to wean me away from my self-appointed role of armchair philosopher of human corruption, "I think she uncovered enough about herself to put her on your Friday night free list" — which put Kathleen on our rather long list of prohibited imports.

So I was startled when Kathleen came through the front door on the next Friday night free-for-all at the Hogans, all dressed up for a party, indeed quite transformed from head to toe. What with the hair neat and tidy and the shoes newly polished, a slattern had been metamorphosed into a well-groomed English lady, making us aware of our own slovenliness of speech and dress and manners, yet saying — the words alone being inconguous with the picture of her at the door — "I was just giving the dog some exercise when I heard all the commotion, and thought I would find out what it was all about."

So I simply had to say, what I had inwardly wanted to say, "Do come in. You're just in time to hear Jimmy O'Donoghoe tell us how he lost his faith in the Philosophy Theatre at the University of Melbourne, and regained it in a Middle East brothel during the war."

"Let me tell you first of all about the young Englishman who told the Madame in a French brothel that he was a virgin. To which the Madame replied, '*Comment, vierge à dix-sept ans? Les Anglias sont drôles.*' That's why I adore the French."

I tried to cap this with my little piece on the human comedy — "I have found that when people say they adore everything French, what they really mean to say is they want to break the seventh Commandment."

"Ah, Mr Hogan," Kathleen replied, eyes slant-wise, savouring words, wine and tobacco smoke, "I see you have what the French call '*une mauvaise Langue*'."

"Ah," I said, "I notice that for Madame words have their uses too."

"Mr Hogan," she replied, half in jest, half in panic, "I'm not sure that I like you."

And so there we were in danger of falling into that trap for intellectuals, of communication by wounding each other.

But I resisted that temptation: something told me to hold back, to refrain from using that particular Melbourne skill.

It was all too obvious what she was doing. Nature had not endowed her with that shape, that eye which suggests to a man that the whole body may be full of delight. Nor had nature painted her with that suggestion of innocence which suggests to a man that what he has lost is not irrecoverable. It all seemed a pretty crude case of seduction by conversation, something for which the mind needed an equivalent in darkness to what the eye needed when there was some flaw in the face of the loved one. I began to wonder whether dear, simple Jimmy knew he was being invited by all the inflaming talk to give up at least temporarily his hopes in the life of the world to come and become, as it were, a convert at least for that night to French cooking.

That, I gather, was how most of the women on the hillside interpreted the night. On the following morning our nearest neighbour, Elsie Tucker, dropped in for a "quick cuppa" as she put it, adding that it would have to be a very quick one because she had to tear back to prepare the rich-brown gravy for the Saturday roast dinner. Elsie, I may say, seriously believed in nature's gentlemen — and had often made it clear that I was not one of them. She had a wonderful way of saying to me, "Charles, I'm terribly fond of Anna. We all are." That conveyed a whole world — as indeed did even the simplest of her remarks convey a whole world by what she left out, and what she added with her eyes, while a disapproving, reproving hum came through her tight lips. As a judge of humanity she reminded me of Calvin's God, though I hasten to add she had not the slightest interest in what happened to us all on judgment day. She just elected some for the drawing-room, and some for the gutter, and never seemed to think human beings wanted any other prize than an entree into a few choice drawing-rooms in Croydon and an invitation to the annual Golf Club Ball.

I had learned years ago to pay no attention to the fluttering eyebrows, which suggested something as delicate and powerless as a butterfly when one should have been thinking of the cunning of the fox.

"I passed Georges on Friday afternoon and saw out of the

corner of my eye such gorgeous crisp cool cottons for this summer's dresses, and would have loved to price their snow-white sheets. Only I didn't dare. Poor Cecil has been so nervy lately — he seems to need so much sherry to calm his nerves that the family has had to go on a very tight budget. The poor dear's still sound asleep. He seems to get so tired if he has to get out of his chair in the weekends. Talking of bed reminds me I must rush, but before I go do tell me what you made of our new neighbour. We all noticed she had a very special interest for you, Charles."

To which my wife, who had either a boundless charity, or no premonition of the murky waters over which Elsie wished us to gloat, said, "I thought she was very gay and lively."

"She was certainly lively," Elsie conceded, stressing the last word, "but gay would not be my word for her — I would think of some word such as 'unsavoury' — though I must admit Cecil and the boys found her very amusing."

"Oh, well, Elsie," my wife said, "it takes all sorts to make a world."

This caused quite a fluttering of the eyebrows, and that toss of the head of a woman at bay, and some measured words through a tiny aperture between thin quivering lips:

"I don't think she is the sort to make up the Brigadier's world when he issues invitations for his Christmas drink."

After she left, I went to the Croydon pub to hear the lords of creation on their sovereign remedy for all the aches of the human heart. To judge by the conversation of the beery boasters in pubs, no one can say we are not a virile nation — at least in intention, if not in performance. No sooner had the drinks been poured than one of the men on our hillside put the question —

"Well, will we put one down first, or start talking about it straight away?"

They laughed. Then another man from the hillside, a renegade from the church, for whom socialism and bed were very pleasing substitutes for the life of the world to come, whispered in my ear, "My God, Charlie, that new woman you had in your house last night is hungry for it. And I've a good mind to give it to her myself."

Perhaps I looked a little sceptical, or maybe just distant, because he seemed quite hurt when he put his question, "Don't you believe I could?"

I wanted to say it was not a question of desire or capacity, but stopped short, because how could I say there, at the very communion rail of Australian mateship, that I had become a doubter, even an unbeliever. How could I say that I was beginning to wonder whether anyone whose bookshelves were covered with the works of Anatole France, with the *Introductory Lectures on Psycho-analysis*, with van de Velde's *Ideal Marriage*, could know very much about the secrets of the human heart. But to have said to anyone of them then, "The heart is deceitful above all things, and very wicked," would have meant excommunication from the church of Australian mateship.

That was a price I was not prepared to pay, because membership of that church was very precious to me at that time. So I held my tongue, though it was great agony to me, and pretended with them that when we took down the mighty from their seat in Australia and sent the rich empty away, everything would be very nice . . . though I wanted to ask whether in any society men and women would ever stop tormenting each other in those cosy cottages under the gum-trees. I belonged to a group who believed that their happiness and their well-being, their innate goodness, had something to do with what happened to the Bank of New South Wales, and the B.H.P.

I remember thinking on the way home from the pub how odd it was that Kathleen, too, had her own explanation for her disquiet. She had told me about it the night before over the post-midnight drinks, when it was clear that conquests were out for the night and booze and pity were all that were left. I gather this left her seething inwardly, rather like a man who is kept well supplied by his wife with orange juice at his first party after his decision to go on the "wagon" for a while to regain his self-respect, only to find his last state, the state of the seethings, worse than the state of being, as the Lord Buddha put it "athirst whilst drinking". Over those post-midnight drinks (I may say she was a sipper rather than a swallower, and quite a novice for someone so strong on *"le bon appétit des hommes*") she had begun to tell her story to me. She was sitting in the old family armchair in which all those gloomy ancestors of mine had talked of their longing for that day when they fell asleep in Christ. She came quickly to the point.

"Papa," she said, "had wanted a boy, and Mama gave him me — *voilà tout*, as the French say."

Perhaps I looked doubtful, as though it was not all.

"You know," I said, "at the University there is a woman. Whenever the world becomes too much for her, she lashes out with her tongue, and then gets one back, which touches her on the raw. There is no one like the Melbourne intellectuals as flagellators of the human heart — Torquemada was a babe-in-arms on the subject of human cruelty compared to them She says in between floods of tears, 'My father was killed at Gallipoli before I was one year old.' "

I wanted to say I was wondering whether this was good enough as an explanation, or pretext, or excuse, call it what you will, for a wielder of the whip.

But she went on to widen the field of explanation: "Papa never forgave me for taking up French instead of learning book-keeping at the local Grammar school in Manchester."

"Yes," I said, warming a little to her as that field of the possible widened, "I believe that men of Manchester believe there is a connection between book-keeping and human happiness" — which won me a smile, a squeeze of the arm, a remark that I was really a most understanding man, and, most important of all, an offer to fill my glass. So when we settled down again, she to look at her drink, the colour of it being more pleasing to her than the effect, and I to swallow mine, the atmosphere had become much more friendly.

"And when I got a scholarship to Oxford —"

"Ah, Madame has the head-piece clever, too."

"You know," she said, "you're not like other Australians — boorish beer swillers, and supporters of organized hooliganism at the football" (I adored both) "— you're kind and gentle and understanding." (This to the one man on the hillside who had tried every remedy for his own swinishness and found them all wanting.)

"I like you . . . I thought I wouldn't at first, but I find I do."

74

(Scholarship boy meets scholarship girl and finds they both know about the fly that feeds on the human heart.)

But I said nothing. So she continued:

"And my tutor at Oxford got me excited about the use of the subjunctive in the fourteenth century. . . . And did that bring out the artist in ridicule in Papa? Do you know what he told me? That if I had had a pretty face, and a good pair of legs, they would have made me an expert on Madame Bovary."

(Oh, my God, I thought, she is going to tell me the story of how this new Emma Bovary, the daughter of Manchester's Mr Money Bags, met her M. Bovary in the tropics — and suffered. So I tried to keep it on a lower level of human activity.)

"Don't tell me," I said, "that you married the first man who told you that you had a pretty face?"

"Well, that's one way of putting it — though there was more to it than that. He was kind: he was understanding: he was so much older than I was."

"Ah," I said, finding it easier to use a bantering tone on such subjects, "so Madame found a sympathetic father and married him."

As she talked I began to see the figure in the carpet of her life — being cursed with that inability to be quiet until I find the figure in the carpet of everyone's life — as though, without a figure, chaos, with its attendant panic and insecurity, would ensue. I began to see Kathleen as one of those women who had sought refuge from a tormentor first in academic pot-hunting, and then in sympathy from an older man. I was beginning to laugh inwardly at the thought: after all, who would have thought the use of the subjunctive in the fourteenth century would have performed such a service? I was even beginning to see Kathleen in a more kindly light, not as someone "unsavoury" as the unhappy women wanted to see her, or as someone who was "hungry for it" as the potency men wanted to see her, but as another one of those women wandering over the face of the earth who in a moment of folly had made some ghastly mistake, and had to live with it for the rest of their days.

So I said to her, probing as it were for the innocent heart which I wanted to find beneath that surface corruption, "I

75

once knew a woman who, on the rebound from a tormenting father, married a man who turned out to be a hitter — and now wants to find someone who can tell her why if she was supposed to be so clever, she was mad enough to do that."

To which Kathleen replied with such a neutral "yes", that I decided to try another example.

"And I once knew a woman who said she would spend her life looking for someone who would not let her down. Well, she married such an earnest man that she is now dying of boredom."

But again this did not touch Kathleen: the fate of others was not her subject: nor the private hell in the heart. So we stopped for that night, though, somewhat to my surprise, Kathleen said to my wife at the door just as she was leaving, "Don't you find it odd to be married to a man whose mind is an attic of human failures? Rather unhealthy, I call it, don't you?"

So perhaps, Kathleen was just another girl from the suburbs whom chance had whisked away for an extended season in the clubs of Singapore, which had smudged her face, but left her suburban heart intact. But there was more to it than that.

She told me how she covered her walls in the bungalow at Bukit-Tingi with prints by the French painters — a nude by Renoir, and one of the Tahitian works by Gauguin. ("Damn," she said, "I always forget what it's called, but you know the one I mean — the one with the man on the horse on the sand — I adore the rich colours — so vibrant with life.") She always carried a set of Marcel Proust with her just to show how tolerant she really was — "Besides," she added, "I like to pour my heart out once in a while to a queer. They really are very understanding, you know, and never censorious. That's what I like about them: they never look as though you should have done anything different — as though you were dirty."

"You mean," I said, "as though someone had muddied your heart."

But again she did not rise to that idea.

The parlour pinks on our hillside (and this decade of the 1940s was so much their heyday that there were quite a few cottages of rest and culture, nestling under the gum-trees on the

76

hill, perfecting themselves in the handicrafts of woodwork and weaving, or warbling away on the recorder. All we believers in the masses were perfecting ourselves in the pursuits of the few — but that is a subject in itself) — the parlour-pinks were always manoevring to see her for their own sport, the exposure of reactionaries. It was a time when there was much talk about the Fascist beasts in the British colonies. But Kathleen dodged and ducked.

"Fascist beast," she would say, *"qu'est-ce que c'est que cela?"* and laugh. "How many times do I have to tell you that politics is not my forte?" And in private she would ask me, "Why do they fuss like that?" I did not know the answer then, except to say that tying up people to a whipping post was a very old Australian sport . . . a rather wild stab at an answer to a problem which had not touched me deeply at that time.

After one of these scenes, I remember asking her why the panic lights had switched on behind her eyes when these wolves were snarling at her, as though they would not or could not stop until they had howled her out of the pack. Her whole face was bathed in pleasure.

"That's such a perceptive remark," she said, "that it deserves a drink."

So while I wondered, wistfully, whether my perceptive powers would come anywhere near the size of my thirst, Kathleen dropped her sewing. It was in the needle-threading moment that one realized one was being pressed to give of one's best. It was always a moment of relief for her to stick the needle into the pin-cushion, throw the material on the floor, stretch herself, and rub her hands with childish glee, as though to say, "Now for some fun."

"Your usual man-size, Charles," she said as she poured out enough drink to quieten that little man inside me who kept saying, "Your wife is right: you revel in stories about corruption — the viler the better."

"It happened to me over in Singapore," she said, "when I was carrying my first child. Cecil, my husband, was too darn stingy to pay my fare back home. The men soon lose interest in you — I only wanted to curl up in myself, and wait for my time . . . I was scared. One of my friends at the Club had told me it was like trying to pass a brick side-ways."

I laughed.

"Oh, yes," she said, "it is rather amusing."

"My Australian friends say it is not as bad as a good kick in the private parts."

"They would, wouldn't they? Trust them — you know we English are the only ones who believe a woman should not let off steam. The Chinese women howl through the whole ghastly business — and so do their relatives who are camped round the bed. The Italians beat their stomachs and shriek, and beseech the Virgin to help them, and generally carry on. Tell, me, my friend, why do we of all people have to pretend the pain is not there? What cruelty is this? It's those blasted puritans, those kill-joys."

I tried to chip in with a remark that there was more to it than that, if we wanted to explain why men tormented each other by allowing the strong to formulate a code which the weak could not achieve and then punish them for their breaches of the code. But that was not Kathleen's subject, that scrutiny of the human heart: she wanted satisfaction, not explanation. So she silenced me: "*Tais-toi, tais-toi,*" she said as those words wiped the smile off her face, and the cloud of some dark memory swept over it; and she slumped right back into her chair, and spoke without animation, like someone stunned by a blow.

"But that's what I could never manage . . . I mean, to keep quiet — I must have screamed. At least, I think I must have, because next morning, when I came to, after the effect of those things they give you had worn off, the Chinese ward-maids giggled when they brought me my first cuppa — God, did I need that? — and the matron, well, it was not so much what she said, she was ever so polite really, she said "Well, and how are we today?": it was the way she looked: it was as though some mongrel had crawled into one of the wards reserved for thoroughbreds. She made me feel I was some bitch who had just been expelled from the tribe of the *gens supérieurs.*"

"Well, just as there is nothing like marriage to soften up the morals, so there is nothing quite like an English matron to make women of imagination feel vile."

"You do say the nicest things."

"And if you offend against the code of one tribe of human beings, you can always join another — unless, of course, you do something which leaves you a vagabond on the face of the earth, a sort of eternal outsider, whom no group will accept."

But the thought of this did not distress Kathleen. She was soon away again on her reminiscences. I always thought of her as the sort of person who took what was in front of her, never wondering whether the evil of one day would haunt her forever: she accepted Christ's remark about sufficient unto the day is the evil thereof — though not for Christ's reason. For her that was all "medieval dirt". I mean all that talk about evil and darkness. She lived for the pleasures of the moment.

"And, you know," she said, "when I began to explore *'les scènes de la vie de Bohême à Singapor'* what delighted me was the number of people who seemed to need me."

"You mean the men?"

"Of course I mean the men, silly. Why should I spend time with my own kind? One of them was going to put me into his next play; another was going to give me a part in his cantata for two voices — it was to be called *Reconciliation*, the reconcilation of man and woman, of east and west in Singapore. It was an idea he wanted to develop during his next furlough in London."

"I suppose," I said with the simple-boy-from-the-country voice, "that some of these friendships became, shall we say, rather warm."

"*Oh, là, là,*" Kathleen replied with child-like pride, "there were stories of queues outside the house — but that was all Singapore lies, or mostly lies. I could count them, you know, on the fingers of one hand — certainly of two hands — though, perhaps, I might need the assistance of some toes to get an accurate score. Mind you, I never count the first time. After all, why chalk up a fiasco? Would you count the first time?"

I wanted to say that I was not in a position to say. I even thought that it might be appropriate to come in with the remark T. E. Lawrence was said to have made about the other Lawrence's *Lady Chatterley's Lover* — that he knew nothing about that subject — thank God! But Kathleen wanted an audience, not a partner in a dialogue.

"They seemed to need me so much."

"You mean they were thirsty, and you gave them drink."

"What a wonderful way of putting it."

"They didn't use that great quotation from that anthology for the seduction of middle-aged ladies: you know, the remark by Benjamin Constant, '*Cela leur fait si peu de mal et à nous tant de plaisir.*' "

"No, not that, silly. How many times must I tell you that they needed me, or said they did."

"And when they asked for bread, you didn't give them a stone."

"Oh, we are getting religious, aren't we?"

"Well, I don't suppose you ever gave out even the faintest suggestion of Christ's 'Touch me not. *Noli me tangere.*' "

"Certainly not — but what can I say about it? *C'est la vie* — at least more like life than what some blasted hypocrites want."

"And what about your husband?"

"That was the cream of the joke: I don't think he knew what was going on."

"Yes — I have always thought Christ should have added a beatitude for wandering wives."

"*Quoi?*"

"You remember. Blessed are the peace-makers: blessed are the pure in heart: blessed are the mourners (He meant, of course, those who were sorry for our great folly). He should have added: blessed are the husbands who do not see."

But, again, I was mistaken in Kathleen. She thought of this, her husband's blindness, as a stroke of fortune to be explained, but not probed.

"You mean," she said, "it's lucky for their wives. But why must you poke round beneath the surface of things? I remember once in Malacca when Cecil took over as acting judge, that composer boy I told you about, you know the one who was going to write the *Reconciliation* cantata, pleaded with me to let him know that peace which passed all understanding — he was really awfully sweet about it. So what with his telling me how much he would suffer if I didn't let him —

telling me this just as my own boy woke up from his afternoon sleep, and called 'Mummy' . . . just as hungry, too, though in a different way — and what with my sweet musician imploring me that it would not take a minute, and the boy calling out again 'Mummy', what could I do but say, 'Yes, but please be quick because you can hear the boy, blast his eyes, so skip that part today about how it makes you feel very gentle with man and beast and get on with the business. Which he did magnificently, because, dear Charles, there are no lovers quite like '*artistes manqués*' — it's their creation. Only I had no sooner told him please to be quick than there was a crash next door and a scream and I rush in to find the chest of drawers had fallen and just missed my boy. It did give me a nasty turn."

"And I don't suppose you ever spoke to your composer again."

"Well, that's the extraordinary turn of fate, you know. He's turned up again. He's here in Melbourne, teaching music at the private schools. In fact, Cecil and I have invited him home on Saturday night for a musical evening. He wants to go over some French pastoral songs with me — thinks I would have just the right sort of voice for it. So do come — I mean bring your wife, too, of course, if she will come. It should be quite amusing. Cecil, you know, is tone deaf."

My wife asked to be excused. She told me, as she had told me so many times before, that she had little patience with this role of observer of human corruption, adding that I could attribute her absence to our little children. Just as I left she called out "Goodbye, and good hunting," which put an edge of desperation onto my mood on first entering Kathleen's drawing-room — that sense of a blemish which had come from eternity and would never change. I was in a mood to respond to the recklessness with which Kathleen conducted her whole life.

There were only four of us in the room. There was Cecil, who apologized for everything — "How awfully stupid of me." He was the perfect "my-fault-entirely" man to whose apologies, self-accusations, and protestations of unworthiness Kathleen responded with more and more abrupt questions and comments. "Cecil, have you given Mr Hogan a whisky?" "No,

Cecil, I thought I told you he does not take water." "No, darling, not two fingers for Mr Hogan, the tumbler full." The composer looked vacuous: he was one of those men who came alive when they play an instrument. After the drinks — "Cecil, you stupid man, you've left Mr Hogan's glass empty."

"Yes, darling, frankly I thought one tumbler would be enough to refresh any man."

"Never mind about refreshment. Just fill his glass, and keep on filling it."

Then she told us, strangely blushing, that she would sing first of all "*Non, je n'irai plus au bois. Je connais trop le danger.*" (That "r" in the "*trop*" would have revved up the coldest of engines in the old days.) In my innocence I wondered if this was a delicate way of telling both composer and me that, as it were, she was going "no more a-roving" by the light of the moon — that that great dynamo inside her had finally wound down.

But, at the end of the song, she fumbled for a cigarette packet on the top of the piano, opened it, found there were none and said, "Blast it. I'm simply dying for a cigarette. Cecil, dear, would you and Mr Hogan be two angels and walk to Mooroolbark and get me a couple of packets of those Benson and Hedges — you know the ones that don't seem to affect my throat."

The two of us set off together in silence. I was just beginning to wonder what it would be like to suffer as he must have done. After all, the only suffering we parlour pinks knew on that hillside was the severe hangovers after the end of the war when we gorged ourselves on cheap gin. Perhaps he would tell me about it — allow me to share some of his pain. The copious draughts of whisky had stirred up that illusion of compassion for everyone.

So it came almost as a let-down when he said, "It's really awfully good of that composer chappie to spend so much of his time with Kathleen. She tells me he was in Singapore before the war, but I can't place him."

I wondered whether perhaps he was just being English, and treating me as a raw colonial, a hayseed who knew nothing of the flies that feed on the human heart. I remember wanting to tell him, "Look here, I am Beelzebub, the lord of the flies," but that thought soon passed, as I began to remember my wife's remark that there was no difference between the actors and the observers of human corruption. There under the gum-trees I understood for the first time why Macbeth had said: " 'Twere best not know myself."

A Democrat on the Ganges

EVERYONE in the University Labor Club agreed that Jack and Val Howell were "naturals" to send on a good will mission to the students of India.

"Let's drink," the president of the club said in his farewell speech, "to a couple of decent democrats, two crusaders of good will, two people who have been behind every good and progressive movement at the Shop for the past five years. Let's drink to two good mates, Jack and Val Howell."

And that is what they were — decent democrats, crusaders of good will, and good mates. Jack had learnt the truth about life in the sociology classes in Melbourne. He was a man who stood for something, a man who knew how to make people better. Not that he was a goody-goody, or sloppy, or unctuous. He sucked all day at his huge cherrywood, sometimes asking his friends, "Do you think I could scrounge a fill of 'baccy, mate?"

Everyone liked Val, too; she had what old-fashioned people called "a sweet nature". What Howell liked about her was her great eyes, and her habit of closing them whenever she said, "As you say, Jack, what this country needs is a few decent democrats."

So when the Club was asked to nominate two people to go to India everyone thought: Who else could it be but Jack and Val?

They were just as popular on the boat from Melbourne to Bombay, where Jack was a "natural" for president of the deck-sports committee, and Val a very good secretary. Bombay and Delhi, however, were a bit of a shock. It was all far more expensive than they had expected. Besides, as Jack put it, they found it hard to get on the right side of the students they met.

"I can't take a trick with these people, Val." What Howell meant was that they looked puzzled or unimpressed when he told them about "the Aussie ideal of being mates".

Howell was a man who needed a programme, needed to be doing things. So after a few gloomy, moody days in Delhi he "nutted out a schedule".

"Look here, Val," he said, "we may as well have a geek at everything while we're here. Why not stop off for a night at Benares on the trip from Delhi to Calcutta, and see the sights on Mother Ganges . . . see the burning-ghats, before decent education and decent conditions give these people an adult attitude to death?"

"That would be wonderful, dear, if . . . only promise not to be cross with me if I say it . . . now, promise?"

"Of course I promise."

"Do you think we can afford it, dear? I've already had to ask my father for more money, and we haven't half-finished the trip."

Howell took the cherrywood out of his mouth, and pointed it at his wife.

"Now look here, dear —"

Two days later Howell and Val arrived at the Old Delhi station, and found the first-class compartment reserved for them. In one hand Howell was carrying his cherrywood. When he wasn't sucking it he found it helped to give weight to his conversation.

Under his other arm he was carrying his reading matter for the journey, a pamphlet on *The Role of the Social Sciences in Underdeveloped Areas* by a reader in sociology at the National University in Canberra. He was still puzzling why some of the students in Delhi found the title offensive — "Rum people, these. You show them the know-how, and they take it from you, but instead of being grateful, they resent it."

A minute or so after they sat down the first hawker arrived with a tray of brightly painted home made toys. Howell thanked him politely for calling, then asked him to leave. The man pretended not to understand: "Sahib buy toys for children?"

Howell spoke slowly and deliberately, spacing his words: "We like your toys; we think they are very good, but we don't need them." Then he smiled — what he called his smile of "democratic benevolence". Still the man did not budge. So Howell tried his brotherhood-of-man gesture: he put his arm round the man's shoulders, thumped him warmly on the back, and laughed what he hoped was a democratic laugh, full of good will and fraternal sentiments; but each thump also had in it a faint suggestion of a shove, which, to his disappointment, only made the hawker dig his heels in. Also, and this bothered him more, the man did not laugh in return, so that the last of Howell's laughs faded into a few nervous er-ars; then dead silence, which the hawker broke by saying in broken English, "You rich man, Sahib . . . I poor man. Sahib buy toys from me."

By Agra they had bought so many extras that Val suggested perhaps they had better buy another bag in Benares — a really big bag, big enough to hold what she called the present takings and anything they picked up between Benares and Calcutta.

"And while we are talking of bags, dear," she went on, "do you think you'll be able to manage to carry our big bag from the train to the bus at Benares?"

Howell looked at his wife long and patiently. "I have told you before, dear, this is India where the buses don't go anywhere near European hotels. And if we have a taxi we may as well have a porter. Anyhow, the poor blighters grab your bag.

But the moment we get to the hotel I'll start showing these Indians the meaning of democracy. I'll carry the bags up to the room. You wait and see."

But as the taxi glided towards the steps in front of the hotel, Howell saw he would have competition for the bag. Three bearers were pacing up and down on the veranda. Behind them, in a European suit, stood the manager. Howell's heart sank.

As soon as the car stopped he jumped out, dropping his pamphlet as he did so, stuffed the cherrywood hurriedly into his coat pocket, bumped his shins on the rear bumper-bar, wrenched the case out of the boot — all this before the bearer had reached the car. The manager then held out his hands to greet Howell, and while they were shaking hands and arranging for Howell to sign the visitor's book a bearer took the case and walked off to the lift with it. . . .

Just before they entered the dining-room after their bath Howell hissed to Val, "If you will insist on talking about money the whole time, make damn' sure you only take food or drink from one waiter. . . ."

One man brought the soup. Val said she liked his turban, but Howell felt so besieged that he dared not look the man in the face, and felt angry with Val for expecting him to behave as though everything was normal. A second waiter asked whether the sahib and the memsahib would like fish, and when the fifth waiter brought the coffee Howell had found the explanation which absolved him from personal responsibility:

"It's all the consequence of concealed unemployment, dear. When you pay a tip to these waiters, and we'll be paying five tomorrow — think of it, *five* — it's not really a tip, it's an unemployment benefit, a tax for welfare. But don't worry, there won't be any of that nonsense on the Ganges tomorrow. We'll have to hire a boat to go out on the river, but, by Jove, I'll row it myself. I don't want slaves to row me about; and, as you say, we can't afford them. We'll tell them I'm just a simple boy from the bush, not a sahib."

The next morning after breakfast they met their guide, a dapper little man with sunglasses, neatly pressed tropical suit, and a spotless white shirt. If you asked a question the reply was like a school lesson, with a striking introduction, development of theme, and recapitulation. As soon as they were seated in the car the guide began:

"In Hindu religion cities are associated with gods. So city of Benares is associated with the Lord Siva. Today I show you city of Benares, sacred Hindu city of Siva. People ask: Why is Benares sacred for Siva? I tell you answer. In Hindu mythology Siva lives in Himalaya mountains, on roof of world. So Siva has bathed in water of Ganga River which come from Himalayas. If a man bathes in Holy Ganga, he is bathed by god Siva, he is washed clean, sins, everything, purified by Ganga. Today I show you people bathing in Ganga. . . . And why do people throw ashes of dead persons into Ganga? I tell you —"

When the guide paused to take breath Howell whispered to Val rather hoarsely, "Now's your chance to tell him who we are. Tell him we're democrats. Tell him I'm not a sahib, I'm just a simple boy from the bush."

They both leant forward on their seats.

"I suppose most of your work is with Americans?"

Like most Australians in Asia, Howell and Val disowned the English and Americans. They thought that as Australians they had a right to disown the Americans and the English, to pose as the innocents, as not responsible for the behaviour of the English or the Americans. They hoped that this would make it possible to be matey, and friendly and nice to Indians.

But, for an Indian, a white man who travels in taxis is a sahib. So the guide was puzzled by Val's remark. And it was only after about three minutes or so that he picked up the drift of her question.

"I see, I see," he said. "You mean they give me big appreciation for my work?"

"Yes."

"Yes, maybe fifty rupees, maybe a hundred rupees."

"Well, we're not Americans."

"Not Americans? Then which country you come from?"

"My husband is a simple boy from the bush."

"A simple boy from the bush? No, I do not follow you."

Howell was beginning to feel like a man discovered in an

obscene position. So in a desperate effort to recover the situation he took over from Val.

"She means we're from Australia."

"Ah, yes, Australians. They know how to show appreciation too. Ah, yes, one of your people in 1951 . . . man with sheep . . . how do you say it . . . yes, thank you, a squatter, his appreciation was two hundred rupees."

"God . . ." Howell muttered, and sank back into the corner of his seat.

"And now," the guide began, "I must explain to you the Hindu word 'Maya'. Hindus believe the world of senses, the world we see, world we touch, world we hear, world we smell . . . this is of no importance . . . in it we can take no pleasure . . . that is why we say Hindu religion is not materialist — not like in west where you boast of your material civilization. Very soon now I take you to the Kashi Vishvanath temple. Outside the temple you see statue of Ganesi. Ganesi is Hindu god with head of elephant on man's body. Why Ganesi have elephant's head? I tell you. . . . In Hindu mythology —"

And away he went on the story of Ganesi and Parvati. By now Howell was so flurried he thought he ought to listen because he was paying for it.

When the car stopped the driver opened the door for Val, the guide for Howell.

"First of all," the guide began, "you must meet temple-priest and he gives you garland."

"And what do we give him?"

"Just a token . . . something small . . . maybe a rupee each."

Howell fingered the money in his pocket. Then Val reminded him of the story of Gandhi and the priest at the Kashi Vishvanath temple:

"You remember, dear, you told me how Gandhi gave him only about a farthing because he said the priests were deceiving the people."

"Yes, dear, but people on a good-will mission can't break Indian conventions."

Howell saw about as much of the temple as a traveller sees from a fast train. Anger with his wife, the humiliations he had suffered, kept distracting him. The guide asked him whether

89

they would like to see the Monkey Temple. Val, wanting to protect him from further humiliations, thinking, too, of more priests with itchy palms, put on her "sweet nature" voice for the guide:

"Well, that's really awfully kind of you, I'm sure," and then she closed her eyes and fluttered her eyelids before continuing. "But really, I don't know whether we ought to. You see, my husband and I . . . we don't believe in God."

"Ah, yes, I remember, your husband, he simple boy from the country."

Howell did not like this. He tried to explain that that was not the reason at all — that he had given up God *after* he had left the bush, but this only made him feel more foolish. So he decided to tell him very few people in Australia believed in God. But the guide seemed even more astounded by this.

"They not believe in God?" he asked. "What then do they believe in?"

Howell found it difficult to tell him. "I'd like to see the Monkey Temple even if my wife doesn't want to," he said. "Take *me* in."

Val, however, had not lost her grip. She was still able to say without bite, "Slip the garland on, dear — it may save a rupee."

But Howell was not at all co-operative. "You don't expect me to wear one of those in the streets?" — and he stamped behind the guide, thinking perhaps a man could enjoy India if he didn't have the nag, nag, all the time. A few minutes later he came out of the temple with a garland round his neck.

Val was still trying to be conciliatory: "Well, dear, was it worth it?"

"If you damn' well insist on measuring the worth of everything by what it costs — well, it cost six — *six* — rupees."

"Six rupees?" Even Val found it difficult to conceal her shock.

"Yes, six — one for the garland, and five for charities. But I didn't begrudge the five — I made the priest promise he would put it into his poor-relief fund."

As the guide shepherded them down the ghats to the boat-sheds past the beggars lolling in the sun, the *sadhus* with their long beards and scanty clothing, he touched Howell's arm.

"Drop something small into a begging-bowl."

"Two annas?"

"Maybe a little more. Maybe eight annas."

Just to make sure it was enough, Howell dropped a rupee into one of the bowls. This brought a swarm of beggars and *sadhus* round him — boys, girls, women of all ages, all holding out a bowl or a hand and chanting, "Sahib, sahib . . ." and looking plaintive or pathetic. This angered Howell. He appealed to the guide.

"Tell those people we are not wealthy Americans!"

"All right, sahib," the guide replied, looking at a boy wearing a filthy shirt with the bottom part in tatters — "I will tell them you are a poor man like them — you have no money for poor people."

This made Howell feel even worse than before.

"Just tell them . . . tell them to *go away!*" And he pointed majestically with the cherrywood towards the Ganges.

The guide coughed and suggested nervously, "If the sahib and memsahib —"

But Howell would not let him finish.

"Look, for God's sake don't call me sahib. It stinks, I tell you, it stinks. Call me Jack."

Howell's heart sank when he saw the boat, especially the two makeshifts for oars, just two flat pieces of deal nailed on to the end of round poles.

"If you don't mind," he said courageously to the guide, "I'll row the boat."

The guide and the two rowers thought this was a huge joke — a sahib rowing a tourist boat on the Ganges. They grinned at Howell, who felt obliged to grin back. The trouble was they continued to grin when Howell began to grunt over the oars, which — trust her to do it — was the very moment Val chose to tell the guide that her husband, her Jack (for Jack he was now, as the guide reminded her) was a famous rower in Australia, that he and seven other rowers, with a special boy to steer them, had won all the races . . . ("Only one, dear") well, not quite all the races in Melbourne, one of the big cities in Australia — almost as big as Bombay. The trouble was the guide could not understand why they needed to have eight men, or why they should row so far. By this time Howell's grunts were so loud they could not be ignored. So Val put her hand on his, imploring him, please, please to be sensible and stop, but Howell, with grunts between each word brushed her hand off, saying,

"A man who has stroked a Head of the River crew . . . I was saying for a man who had stroked a Head of the River crew . . . this is a pushover!"

"Yes, but you should be seeing the sights, dear."

"I've told you before . . ." (long pause) "compared with the Head of the River —"

Soon the boat simply did not move when he rowed.

"I'm flogged, dear." And he lay down plumb in the centre of the boat, breathing like a frightened fish in a rock-pool. Way, way in the distance he could hear the voice of the guide: "Hindus like to die on Ganga. And why do Hindus like to die on Ganga? I tell you. All Hindus believe if they die on Ganga their souls go 'straight to Paradise'. . . ."

What poppycock, Howell was thinking. No wonder your towns are a bloody disgrace to humanity, and most of your people look as though their clothes haven't been washed for a year. What this country needs is not food or foreign experts, but a great huge cake of soap.

Before he could put the idea to Val the guide bent over him with his lips almost touching his ear. That was another thing he had against this bloody country — this physical intimacy from the men: it made you feel you had got mixed up with a pack of queens.

"When the boat come back to bank, sahib . . . so sorry, I mean Jack . . . you pay the rowers, just a little appreciation. . . ."

Howell groaned.

Monologue by a Man in Black

Do you remember Charles Hogan, the man who thought all men of good will were on his side? You must remember him at Melbourne University in the thirties telling his fellow-students the only hope for the world lay in a synthesis of Christ and Freud and Marx. Well, that little swine, you do remember him, with the freckles, always patting his wavy hair with his right hand, and his left hand always plunged deep in his pocket — of course you remember him — well he turned up in Canberra towards the end of the war to teach politics to the cadets in our Department of External Affairs. And now the silly little goat has written a pamphlet saying he and his bosom friend John Flanagan were the victims of political reaction, with me, Grant Polkinghorne, playing the sinister role of *éminence grise*. Of course that idea came straight from my colleague — or rather my ex-colleague — John Flanagan, who I am glad to say is no longer with us in the Department.

You remember Flanagan too in Melbourne in the thirties, another product of an institution which seemed to exist mainly to convert theological students into rationalists, parlour pinks and free lovers. You remember him surely, short, stocky, jet black hair, spruce and tidy, teeth as clean as the enamel in the bathroom here, clean in body but not in mind. You must remember him.

Fancy having to defend myself against a man like John Flanagan. Great Scott, the man has left his vomit on the porcelain of almost every embassy in Canberra. Fancy me — Grant Polkinghorne — having to argue against a common two-pot drunkard — me, slandered by a hopeless drunken sot. But what else can you expect in a society where if you're rude to the milkman you won't get any milk?

And Hogan! Well that's the limit. But does anyone in Canberra take Hogan seriously? Fancy in this year of grace 1954 telling educated people that ours was a tragic age, because we wanted to believe — we could not bear unbelief — but were ashamed of belief. And fancy telling a group of students that the hearts of men are filled with evil, and madness is in their hearts while they live and after that they go to the dead; and that if he taught history he could make it a record of human evil. What sort of mind has a man got who talks about belief and about evil? Only queers go on in that way. I call it damned unhealthy and I'm going to say so.

Anyhow I for one am not taken in by Hogan's claim that he had broken with the Left. The talk about belief is just a thin veneer over the old socialist poison, and damn' thin too, in fact so thin that the poison keeps oozing out. He is cunning enough to cut out all references to his early career as a teacher in Melbourne when he radicalized a whole generation of students. The Security files are chock-a-block full with the names of his ex-students. What a cheek to pose now as a simple, muddle-headed fellow, tortured by the problem of belief — to put it out that all men of good will went Left in the thirties and to Rome in the fifties — as though the desires of his heart should be the measure for all men. One day, if the pressure of other work allows it, I'm going to write a treatise about the hearts of these men of good will. I saw them at work in Australia in the late thirties and early forties and I'm not going to let them start again if I can help it. The people with minds

94

like sewers — the Jews and the intellectual riff-raff — they were the ones who did the damage. They smeared reputations, put the lowest possible motive on every political action and related every event — yes, even the most innocent event — to some deep-seated plan to let the rich get richer and the poor poorer.

I remember Hogan himself once telling me that the worst crime of the men of the Left was to fill the people with false hopes, to delude them into believing that happiness was possible in this world. Frankly, I couldn't care less what the people believe — except of course insofar as it affects their attitude to the rest of society. And I'm not going to let that particular sort of mud-slinging start again. Anyhow, by the time Security has finished with Flanagan he'll think twice before he slings any mud again.

It's not difficult to pick up information in our Department. Give us a child until he is seven, the Jesuits used to boast — and I say, give me a fellow-traveller on a hangover, and I'll worm anything out of him. The guilt of the fellow-travellers makes them rival the Irish as the best informers in the world. And our Department is full of them. It still stinks to Heaven with the smells they left us as a legacy, our reminder of the days when THEY ran the show, and now the only use they serve is to keep US in the picture about the comi-comms, the parlour pinks and secret Stalinists.

A fellow-traveller told me all about Flanagan and Hogan. He told me because he wanted me to know he was a more responsible type than they were; that, although he dis-approved of the trend of events, unlike Flanagan and Hogan he did not drink with the Russians or sign peace petitions or shoot his mouth off about ending nuclear tests, or make Flanagan's mistake of assuming that all men of good will were on the Left, let alone his arrogance, his bigotry in not recog-nizing the right of others to decide for themselves . . . because as he (the fellow-traveller) put it, it was really a sign of maturity, of being an adult, not attributing the worst possible motive to every action. I felt quite queer while the fellow was making this last point. Do you know I think he was flirting with me, yes, damn it, the fellow was touting for affection almost down on his knees begging to be accepted, but I wasn't going to give him that satisfaction. So I said: "I see," and looked at him as though he, not Flanagan and Hogan, were on trial, and tapped my pencil on the table, and said nothing, absolutely nothing, until he left the room in great confusion. Soon I trotted down to see the Head of the Department, and told him we ought to give Security a buzz about Flanagan and the Russians, and while they were on the line get them to frighten hell out of Hogan for signing peace petitions.

But how in the name of fortune can Hogan pose as a martyr to political reaction? I remember the man saying to me once that the Left was finished in Australia, that anyone who still believed that a change in social conditions would improve human beings was a Darling Dodo of the twentieth century. Yet when we are forced, as an economy measure we didn't like, to stop him teaching the diplomatic cadets, he immediately runs off to the people on the Left and poses as the man who lost his job (it was only part of his job anyhow) because he didn't believe in a Yankee war and wasn't afraid to say so. And if anyone starts trotting out this modern psychology tripe to explain or condone his behaviour — this balderdash about our "anxiety-ridden society" — I shall scream. I'm old-fashioned enough to believe in moral responsibility. I hope the Stalinists like it when Hogan takes a glass of neat whisky in one hand — if it is after midnight it will be a tumbler full — and a volume of Dostoevsky in the other and drops on his knees and tells them the first thing they have to do is to fall down on their knees and confess they are murderers.

As for Flanagan — the Stalinists will use him for their own purposes and then kick him into the gutter as a drunkard and a degenerate. The Security people will see that he's turned down from every responsible job in Australia. He knows already that he can't get another job in the Public Service. He'll find out soon that the Universities are too afraid to offer a job to anyone with the reputation of being a "security risk" — and so are the schools. I remember Hogan once saying to me, "Be kind to Flanagan — spiritually he's a sick man."

That was shortly after the big change in Hogan. But the change didn't stop him pontificating about people. "We should be sorry for Flanagan," he said, "he is a victim of the secular humanists with their idea that everything is allowable, and their theory of the mind as a *tabula rasa* at birth — a clean slate on which environment writes every man's character." All stuff and nonsense of course, and I told him so at the time. No, anyone who has the misfortune to listen to Flanagan for five minutes can see what's wrong with him. I see John Flanagan as essentially a weak character — so weak that he let his mind be warped by the foul ideas put round in Melbourne after the First World War by Bohemians, Jews, pacifists, socialists, anarchists and communists. Those social derelicts perverted the minds of a whole generation in Australia. They got their ideas into the schools, the universities, the newspapers — as you know, even clergymen used the pulpit to propagate the poison. They ridiculed the thrifty, the frugal, the industrious, sneered at the successful, and of course they vilified the rich. Flanagan soaked up this drivel in a big way. Every time I hear men in our Department waxing enthusiastic about the Colombo Plan I smell the sewers of the thirties.

Thank the Lord I have never been seduced by any such piffle. Yes, when the testing-time came at the University, I'm proud to say: Polkinghorne stood firm. I don't doubt these gutter-minded friends of Flanagan's have some lavatorial explanation of their own for this — something about my performance on the potty as a baby. That's the other great lie of Flanaganism, that if we all published the results of our anal eroticism in the nursery we would all be nicer to each other — that he wouldn't puke his vomit on to the porcelain of the embassies in Mugga Way, and I would stop kissing the arse of the masters.

Frankly I couldn't care less when I decided to offer my services to preserve the established order. I drifted into this position just as naturally as Flanagan flowed towards the people with a taste and a talent for destruction. If you want to know what makes society· tick just watch school-masters, parsons, university lecturers and public servants — I mean watch the way they tie themselves in knots between social ideals, ethos, all the philanthropy and duty and Boy-Scout ideas of service, and the sludge of religious teaching on equality, all those influences which fashion the conscience of the servers of mankind — I watched them years ago tie themselves in knots between conscience and inclination and decided on a simple remedy: don't tie the knot.

And what vermin those young Lefties were at the Melbourne University in the thirties. I remember once in the Refectory, which they of course called the Caf, I was praising Signor Mussolini for rescuing Italy from complete anarchy, and saying that firmness was essential to save the whole of Western Christendom from *stasis*, when the vermin bared their teeth. Another time, at a table at which the vermin predominated, I was incautious enough to discuss the magnificent recovery the British had made from the trough of the depression and said what a masterstroke it was to introduce the ten per cent cut, and that there hadn't been anything like it since the Seisactheia by Solon. I said you couldn't expect anything so statesmanlike here from State-school swots and Christian Brothers' products whose brains were as transparent as the alpaca coats of their teachers — that uneasy alliance of mediocrities which made up the civil service in Canberra. This time they enjoyed the joke rather than take exception to the political point I had made, because I had stooped to their level. I had become a mocker.

Some of the vermin from Melbourne followed me to Canberra in 1938 when I took up a billet in the foreign service. While cutting my teeth in the service I blundered a little. At first I prattled too freely after a few sherries — and uncovered myself in a rather unguarded way. I remember one rather indiscreet performance of mine in a drawing-room where I told the company that Canberra society could be divided into heavy-weights and light-weights, and I proposed to take my apéritifs with the heavy-weights. I knew the vermin were in town when I heard what became of that remark!

My dress, too, made the plebs gnash their teeth, and Flanagan's team of rabble-rousers stir the sludge. I used to wear morning coat, striped trousers and spats to official receptions. Flanagan, I am told, excelled himself when he first heard of it. "Trust that queen to wear gloves on his feet," he said. But, thank God, none of these indiscretions was irredeemable — not like Flanagan's. I learnt quickly how to climb the slippery pole of preferment and had just managed to get my feet well off the ground when a dreadful thing happened. War was declared.

Soon the most odious people began to turn up at parties and receptions at the Hotel Canberra. The war seemed to exist to give jobs to economists and political scientists with one of those dubious doctorates from the London School of Economics. I was surprised to find such people existed in Australia, surprised to learn too in September 1939 that to clean up the mess left by democrats, liberals and socialists, the Germans, in sheer desperation, had risked using the services of a gifted megalomaniac. Why every man with a classical education knows that the health of the body politic cannot be restored by those methods. Haven't the Germans heard of Peisistratus and Marius?

I had always thought of myself as in some sense a missionary for gracious living in Canberra. Alas. At the end of 1941 the Government fell. "Put away your crystal and your sterling silver," I said that night to my wife, "they won't be wanted again for a generation." The very next day, to confirm the accuracy of my prophecy, I heard that the new Minister had appointed one of those graduates from the London School of Economics to be Head of the Department. A man not lacking in talent, but crude and just as bankrupt of ideas as Flanagan, and like all those Fabians, blast their eyes, obviously itching to take control of us — body and soul. The dark thoughts which crossed my mind at the time were confirmed when I heard that Flanagan had given a party to celebrate the event, and our new Head was his guest of honour. Just my luck that the first ukase of this czar of our lives applied to dress:

> In future all officers will refrain from wearing dinner suits at gatherings where they are representing the Department.
>
> H. Baker,
> *Secretary.*

I roared with laughter when I read that note. Fancy a scholarship boy, a son of a State-school teacher, imagining that he could change correct dress by the stroke of a pen.

Anyhow I began, well not exactly to swim with the tide, but shall we say, to float along with it. I made concessions. I wore a belt instead of braces, a soft instead of a stiff collar, and occasionally, though only very occasionally, I undid the buttons of my coat when walking from the office to lunch at the Hotel Canberra — but I drew the line at open-neck shirts and walking with the coat slung over the arms, or, as I regret to say of our new Head, without any coat at all.

I was a fool however to make any concessions to those barbarians. I was a butt for all their jokes. Everything in the Department had to be genuinely Australian — the paintings on the wall, our speech, sentiments, even our prose style.

I remember submitting a memorandum to the Secretary on the future of the Dutch possessions in the East Indies, early in 1944. I used the traditional language of diplomacy, something like this: "I have the honour to inform you," my memorandum began, "that His Majesty's Government in the United Kingdom has certain reservations about any transfer of sovereignty in the islands adjacent to Australia at the conclusion of hostilities. . . . "

Well, the Secretary slashed my chaste page with a blue pencil, and wrote in an almost illegible scrawl across the top: "Cut the claptrap, Polk, and tell us what you think of those Dutch Fascists."

All these people lavished praise and admiration on the Russians with as much discrimination and discernment as a bitch on heat. They sneered at America as the land of comics and gangsters. They patronized the English as representatives of the graveyard of liberal civilization, the prelude to their perfect society.

This association with the Russians caused me endless embarrassment. In the last quarter of 1944 the Soviet Embassy in Canberra held one dreary party after another to celebrate their victories in Europe. I just could not share the elation of the hoi polloi, though of course I always dropped in for the odd half-hour strictly according to protocol. Flanagan, I need hardly mention, was in his element. "Be in it Polk," he said to me before one party, "the drinks are free even if you don't like the company."

And what a shambles that party was! Tobacco smoke was weaving round the imitation crystal in the chandelier when I arrived. As I shook hands with the ambassador I bowed low and murmured, *"Mes félicitations, votre Excellence."*

Out of the corner of my eye I could see Flanagan with a glass of vodka in one hand, a long Russian cigarette between his lips and another tucked behind his ear (cigarettes were precious currency at the time — even my tobacconist in Sydney had had to cut my quota). He made his way in an unsteady line towards me, holding his glass by the stem, with the vodka spilling out. I winced when he licked his wrist. "Come on Polk," he said, swaying on his heels. "Come on, you old sod, let's drink a toast together to the greates' man of all time — Joe Stalin — the only friend the working man ever had."

"Thank you John, old boy," I said, "but perhaps we had better leave it to our hosts to propose the toasts."

"Oh," he said, trying unsuccessfully to be icily dignified, "so you don't want to drink with me. All right, all right. Eh, Hogan, where's my friend Charles Hogan? — eh, Charles, come and have a drink."

Hogan was a bit under the weather too, and wanted everyone to sing. This was still the period when drink made Hogan sloppy and affectionate. "Come on," he said, "let's sing that bit from the Ninth Symphony, you know, *Alle Menschen werden Brüder. . . ."*

"No, no, not that bullsh," said Flanagan, "let's teach our friends the Russkis that song about Menzies. Come on, you bastards, let's sing that song about Big Bob and the depression."

I closed my eyes, and said to myself: "How long, O Lord, how long?" and, by God, I'm ashamed to say, even senior members of the Department took up the filthy song:

> *Menzies loves us, this we know,*
> *For the* Argus *tell us so,*
> *The unemployed to him belong:*
> *They are weak but he is strong.*

The singing of the chorus was even more ragged and raucous than the verse, and I noticed our hosts looked scared, glanced furtively at each other, and managed a watery smile, a very watery smile.

"Canaille, canaille," I said to myself under my breath, and moved into another room just in time to see one of our Labor old-timers, you know the type, with the stomach almost reaching to the knees, grog blossoms all over his face, and a cheap brown suit covered in front with food stains. He had his arms round the shoulders of a frightened little Russian, saying to him in his wheezing manner, "Listen, I want to ask yer a serious question, that is providin' yer don't mind." But our Labor man didn't wait for permission. "Tell me comrade, why is it, why are yous Russians so crook on God?"

There was a lot of boisterous laughter after that, and as I made my way back into the other room thinking that at least John Flanagan was quite pleasant to look at, I could hear the old Labor member protesting to the others: "No, fair dinkum, I'm serious about this, fair dinkum. . . ."

I arrived back in the other room in time to hear Flanagan bawl out, "Christ, my glass has been empty for too long. Isn't any of you bastards going to fill it up?"

"Jesus, sorry John, I didn't know your glass was empty," and one of our younger men poured vodka into the glass, on to his hand and the carpet.

"Thanks, mate," Flanagan said, tottering on his heels like some drunken beast.

That word "mate" sickened me. I went up to the Ambassador to pay my respects. I could only manage a formal, "I must thank Your Excellency for such a stimulating evening."

These were the days of unleavened bread for me. For who could have foreseen at the end of 1944 that within ten years we should scatter our enemies like chaff before the wind — that we should have the more voluble of those Australians at the Soviet Embassy party up for public inquisition and the rest of them trembling in their shoes wondering whether they would be called?

Now believe me, no one foresaw this at the end of 1944. Why even now at the beginning of 1954 I have to rub my eyes to make sure it's true. Only last night when I was skipping up the steps of the Hotel Canberra I remembered with horror that night ten years before when the planners were holding what they called one of their "shivoos". It was one of those ghastly gatherings where men with red ties and dirty finger-nails guzzled, yes, literally guzzled drinks, told dirty stories (not witty stories mark you, but excretal stories, filthy stories) and competed with each other in vilifying the members of the Opposition, the leaders of the church and the owners of our large metropolitan newspapers. Nothing was safe from those mockers — nothing sacred. I remember Hogan telling me later that men without reverence were not likely to improve the world. What worried me was that in their attempts to improve the world, everything which gave me pleasure — courtesy, breeding, elegance — would go.

I wondered then whether I could live another day with men who thought civilization meant putting a sink in every farm kitchen, and a rest room for women in every factory — men who dreamt of a day when the workers would spend every lunch hour in a hall for rest and culture instead of studying racing form or picking up tips on how to lower the pants of their neighbours' wives.

And by God they meant it. I've seen the plans, the blue-prints as they called them, of these architects of perfect societies, these men with the modest ambition of making everyone happy. Thank God, by then my days in their company were numbered. The secretary at last told me they had decided to send me to London. And I was so relieved that I found it funny when he made a crack that this would give me a chance, as he put it, "to wear my glad rags". Everyone knew I had bought court dress shortly after my marriage. In fact the scurrilous always called it *fructus primae noctis*.

And what a joy London was! Here, instead of that depressing Canberra scene where young men with hexagonal glasses and badly-fitting suits buttonholed you at parties about such dreary subjects as the effect of fluorescent lighting on industrial fatigue, we found people interested in good clothes, good food and good wine. We found, at last, a nanny for the children, and servants who were prepared to serve dinner at eight o'clock, instead of that mad rush at six-thirty when people wolf their food in the same way as they have already swilled their beer before the bars close at six o'clock, because the servant has some wenching appointment at the pictures at seven-forty-five.

Yes, London washed the taste of Canberra out of our mouths.

After the change of Government at the end of 1949 I was recalled to Canberra. I flatter myself that this was because it was realized that my skill and experience were needed for cleaning up the mess of subversion within the Department. Picking Reds was a hobby of mine. My method was quite simple. In general anyone who tries to improve the condition of the workers is either already a Red, or likely to become one. You can be sure too that anyone who has studied history, politics or philosophy at Melbourne is red at heart. The only exceptions to this are those who go to Mass on Sunday mornings and I have known even these to be tainted. For heaven's sake don't be misled by the Student Christian Movement people: they're riddled with the poison. So are all those who've been to the London School of Economics; and, though it pains me to have to say it, even the Modern Greats men at Oxford are not always free from it. Oh yes, in passing, I must mention the supreme importance of finding out the subjects of their university theses. I once removed a man from Top Secret work on our Russian files when I found out that he had written a thesis on "the working classes in New South Wales between 1883 and 1900". I'm glad to say even the most sceptical acknowledged the wisdom of my action two years later when Security told the Head of the Department to label him a security risk.

Of course John Flanagan spread the story round Canberra that all my ideas came from the Americans, and particularly from my friend Sam Chandler on this subject. Oh, I think he said something about stopping people from discussing foreign policy — but I didn't need any hints on that subject. I've always thought that discussion was the secret weapon of the Reds — their way of sowing doubt and confusion.

By the end of 1953 I had compiled a dossier on every member of the Department — dossiers which I kept under lock and key in the bottom drawer of my filing cabinet. I suspected all along that the Head of Security had a pretty shrewd idea there was such a collection, because I was able to tell them exactly when Sebastian Sedgwick resigned from the Executive Committee of the Council against War and Fascism, and the month when

John started to go to a psychiatrist just to see whether he could stave off the attacks of hysteria which incidentally I also knew had a long history. So it didn't come as a complete surprise when the Head of Security rang me in January of 1954 and asked me to meet him at — of all places — Cooma. You know, that place at the foot of the Australian alps.

I'm not going to give you all the details of our conversation. He wanted me to tell him all I knew about the contacts between the members of our Department and the Russian Embassy in Canberra. I felt like a student who had been asked his favourite question in an examination paper. But that was nothing to my excitement a few months later when the Prime Minister announced the appointment of a Royal Commission into Russian Espionage in Australia. I rushed over to Sam Chandler to tell him the news. That was the night he showed me what Hogan had been writing about me.

At first I was livid and almost lost my grip: "Fancy being put in the dock by that Holy Joe!" I said. But after a while the bourbon spread its glow all over my body, and I said to Sam in a quieter tone, "Do you know, Sam, what that Hogan once had the infernal cheek to say to me? He said that Flanagan couldn't stop — that he was driven by tremendous forces, that we should pity him, rather than torment him by asking him to achieve standards he could not possibly observe."

I felt an even warmer glow when dear old Sam told me not to let the blighter shoot me that crap, because, he said, you and I stand for something, though come to think of it, he said, I'm durned if I can put it into words. So I suggested decency, and Sam said, "And the independence of the judiciary," and I said, "And the spiritual values of our civilization," and Sam said, "And among these rights are life, liberty and the pursuit of happiness." And I said, "I believe in human dignity." And Sam said, "And I believe that government of the people by the people and for the people will not disappear off the face of the earth." And I said, "True enough, but what if the Flanagans corrupt the people? . . ." Then Sam, for once, looked pained: "Grant," he said, "don't soil our credo with his name. . . ." Then there was silence, and after a while Sam said, "We seem to have run out of ideas. . . ." And I said, "Yes, but we know what we stand for even if we can't put it into words."

And Sam said, "Sure," and then we both looked at each other and laughed.

The Love of Christ

IF YOU stroll down one of the asphalt paths which radiate out from the University of Malaya on the top of the hill you might think for a moment you were in Europe — an illusion which is heightened if you decide to enter one of the flats at the foot of the hill. For there the eye can rove over the material strength of Europe — the electric light, the refrigerator, all the gadgets to protect man against heat and cold and hunger and thirst. The eye can rove too over the symbols of Europe's spiritual sickness. They are on every shelf, miniature statues of Buddha, of Siva, the strident titles on the spines of the books, all those digests of the world's religions, and those anthologies designed to produce quiet minds.

I was sauntering down one of these paths one sultry Sunday afternoon in January 1956, wondering whether to drop in on Cecil Porter who lived at Keppel Harbour. The trim lawns of coarse grass on either side of the path, the cultivated flower-beds, the clipped shrubs, had nudged my mind towards Europe as a refuge from this garish light and the oppressive heat.

Perhaps there would be a chance to talk about something which had been on my mind ever since we had arrived in Singapore a few months earlier, an uneasy sense of our future doom, a fear that we might be that third or fourth generation of Europeans on whom the sins of the fathers were to be visited.

I knew Cecil would enthuse if I raised the subject with him. In his own way he had quite a special knowledge of human cruelty. Yet I hesitated about bothering him because I knew the subject would strain him. I had known him quite well years ago at the University of Sydney when he was studying to become a teacher. I had first met him shortly after the accident on that hot, blustery westerly-wind day in January of 1932 when a car knocked him down as he was crossing George Street. This branded him for life. I am not thinking of the marks on his body, only heaven knows they were bad enough — one lame leg, the thinning hair, the deep dark furrows ploughing their way through the fresh cheeks, leaving the tops of the cheeks puffy, with great bags of blue flesh forming under both eyes. I'm thinking of the new loneliness of those who are surrounded by people anxious to help.

I remember first seeing him in the cafeteria at the University in 1933, sitting at a table with three other students — Dick Shaw who had a harelip, Eric Miller, a man with a high-pitched laugh, and Margaret Sudholz who was so fat she could not tuck her legs under the table when she was sitting down. But from where I sat you could hear people speaking about Cecil as they passed by. "There's Cecil, marvellous chap; must have a talk to him some day" or greeting him warmly: "Good to see you, Cec, we must have a long talk one day, a really good chin-wag. I'm terribly sorry I can't stop now."

But of course, as I found out later, they never did. At least the normal ones never did, while the "odd fish" as he called them swarmed round him like flies on a fisherman's back. Sometimes a woman in the Student Christian Movement shared a minute with him, pulling a chair up close to his. She would grip the back hard with her long bony fingers and move her head towards him, searching him all over with large wondering eyes, whispering, while holding his hands under the table:

"But how are you, Cecil? I mean really . . . how are you, in yourself?"

At first he accepted the invitation to their weekly prayer meetings with the opportunity, as they put it, to talk things over in an atmosphere of Christian fellowship. For a while he liked it, because he believed he might find there the strength to tell them how he felt in himself. These were the days of promise, his early days in the Movement, but they did not last for long. After a while he began to feel uneasy, to dread the weekly gathering for Christian fellowship, because he wanted to talk about himself as a relief, but they, the other members, the normal ones, the unmarked ones, used this as the beginning, the raw material for their work, their subterranean satisfaction, which was to tell others how to behave. And it was all this advice, this criticism — this "Do try, Cecil, you'll find it worth it," or, at the other extreme, this "I feel we ought to feel intensely proud that God has chosen Cecil Porter to teach us the meaning of Christian suffering" — all this harping on the need not to feel resentment — that made him feel he was being bullied, where he wanted love and understanding and indulgence.

Besides, why should he be accountable to them? Who gave them authority over him? Then there was all the talk about love and about loving your neighbour as yourself, and about loving the black man because he was our brother too, about the love of Christ which made it possible for us, all of us, to love everyone. Week after week they talked about love, gushed about it, raved about it, while he sat there a vessel of hatred, of resentment and anger, wanting their pity, not all their talk about divine love and improvement. The thought of the weekly meeting became a nightmare.

It was Eric Miller who urged him to go to Christ Church, the Anglo-Catholic church opposite the railway station. Eric was one of those young boys with soft down on his cheeks and a girlish laugh who used to sit with him for hours in the cafeteria talking about sin and damnation, and the prots, and all the harm they had done, and his hatred for the Hanoverian upstarts, and how he burned a candle every year on the altar at Christ Church on the feast of Charles the Martyr, and how he loathed this protestant money-bag civilization in Sydney and wanted to put the Stuarts back on the throne, and then there would be a decent legal code, a code a man could respect and not this present money-bag, Jew-boy code for the greedy and the brutal which made it possible for the prots, the Jew-boys, the swindlers and the wanglers to fill their money-bags while people like himself could be put into jail for fifteen years just because they were like Shakespeare and Marlowe, and James the First, and even Christ himself. But these prots, these bullies, who confounded religion and morality, these upright men who drove the nails into our hands every day, because after all they had no need of Christ-like love and compassion since they did not know what it was to suffer — they did not need comfort for their ordeal, because no mark of Cain was stamped on their brows. . . . Not like you and me, dear boy, not like you and me, as he used to wind up his talks to Cecil. He believed these talks were motivated by a sort of companionship of those who bore the mark of Cain, but he wandered off into mockery to ease his own ache.

Cecil did not know what he was talking about, except when he spoke about the ordeal, though he did not know why Eric should complain — he looked all right. A great deal of what he had to say made him feel queer, even dirty, and he wanted to wash himself all over afterwards. Still, Eric did persuade him to go to Christ Church. There he found the comfort, the strength he was looking for. He loved the dim light in the church, because then even the bags under the eyes felt lighter. He loved to hear one of the priests read from the New Testament in his soft musical voice, especially the lesson which ended with the verse: "In the world ye shall have tribulation and sorrow, but be of good cheer, I have overcome the world."

A reverent hush would come over the whole church after he said that, and Cecil would lean forward with lips pouted in expectancy, with the left hand holding on to the seat in front just to make sure he was not the last to stand for the *"Nunc Dimittis"*. Then there were those moments during the responses which contained a message for people afflicted like him — when the high falsetto voice of the priest warmed his heart:

O Lord, make clean our hearts within us.

Here was the great challenge for him, someone singing in an ineffably sublime way about his subject: How to keep the heart clean from resentment, how to stop burning himself out in self-pity, how to forgive others their happiness, those who were not like him, the normal ones, the ones without the brand of Cain. He once told me in a moment of great happiness that he used to rub the mark with his fingers during the responses. But sometimes in the dim light of the church he was not even aware of the mark. A miracle happened: he felt whole, and the anger, the hatred drained out of his heart, he felt clean. Here in the church he could sing about what he wanted. One day he would shout it out in public, he would shout it out to all those cruel people in the University cafeteria, the ones who always said they were going to speak to him but never did. Only Christ could keep the heart clean. Here, with fervour, he could join in the response:

> Because there is none other that fighteth for us but only Thou, O Lord.

He liked the sermons too, or rather some of them. He was bored when a cloud of anger passed over the priest's face as he told them of their great privilege to belong to the true Catholic Church, not the Roman branch, the men "who had corrected Christ's work." After all, what was Christ's work except to make clean our hearts within us? Was not the Christian message one of charity and the love of God? So why waste words as this priest seemed to revel in doing, in warning them about the whore of Babylon, or at the other extreme, against the proud and stiff-necked who pinned their faith in private judgment, in their own puny, frail reason, to work out the way to salvation. He was indifferent too when the priest preached about damnation, because what did it matter to him if the damned were tortured in hellfire? That did not help him. He thirsted for eternity, yearned, strove for the day when "this corruptible shall put on incorruption". That was what he wanted. He raced through the early parts of the Creed, to that great promise in the last paragraph:

> And I look for the resurrection of the dead, and the life of the world to come. Amen.

As with most people whose faith had performed the miracle

of making the world bearable, nightmare speculations about eternity did not visit him either by day or by night. He never startled himself with a question such as, What if all the ones in the Church were raised just as they were? — the crooked crooked, the halt halt, the blind blind? What if, in eternity, too, these women in the Student Christian Movement kept looking at him?

No such doubts, no such anxieties ruffled his faith.

He would tell those cruel women in the Student Christian Movement what he affirmed. He would sing it to them:

And I look for the resurrection of the dead and the life of the world to come. Amen.

Perhaps that would make them stop. Anyhow, what did they know about his great moment, the moment when he wanted to smile in recognition to anyone near who would understand? And surely those near him in the Church must all understand, because otherwise why bother to attend?

He could smile now, feel gentle and tender with everyone, even with the ones who had tormented him. Yet he knew that without this experience, without this love of Christ, the whole world, every living person, every living creature would become loathsome to him. Disgust, that is what he felt without Christ, disgust and loathing, the mind feeding on these poisons. Yet knowing it was true — what St Paul said: "He that hateth his brother abideth in death" — knowing that, feeling that, oh God how to escape that, because without Christ, that was how he felt. He felt in his bowels the great truth of his warning: "He that is angry with his brother without cause shall be in danger of hellfire." He knew that to be true, because until he had come to Christ Church he had been living in Hell.

And even with Christ, even with his love, something still bothered him. There was Christ, but no one else, that is to say no one else came near him. They still passed him by with that wave, that hurried, embarrassed, "Hello, Cecil, must have a talk one day." In between there was no one, or rather only the queer ones, the ones with a mark of Cain, the branded ones. So there he was, with Christ between him and bitterness, between him and that other death, the second death, waiting, watching, yearning for the resurrection of the dead and the life of the world to come. Christ had replied to the great yearning, the yearning for a clean heart, and renewed a right spirit within him.

Each week the miracle happened: the anger, the loathing drained out of him as the service went on in the dim religious light of Christ Church until by the Creed he was ready — ready for the great experience, the renewal as the priest with a wavy voice intoned those words:

I be-lieve. . . .

A wave of love for everyone surged up inside him. He saw beauty everywhere, on the faces of the people around him. His body ceased to be vile, something to be hidden — Christ, the love of Christ, worked the weekly miracle in his heart.

That happened every Sunday — a spiritual refreshment, which had to sustain him through the week. Strong on Monday — fading, fading Tuesday . . . the old loathing and disgust back by Wednesday . . . the heart hungry by Thursday, wanting to tell someone, anyone, except the ones he knew — "I'm hungry for Christ" — till separation, deprivation became unbearable and in agony of incompleteness he lived through Friday and Saturday, waiting for his one relief, that moment when the priest in a wavy voice intoned:

I be - lie - ve. . . .

And the tears of joy welled up behind his eyes, and spilt over on to the cheeks, and the words choked in his throat for very joy as he, with all the others, joined in the words:

. . . the Father Almighty maker of Heaven and Earth. . . .

He wanted to tell someone about this precious gift. . . . But with whom would he begin? Not with those cruel people in the University cafeteria, the ones who passed him every day, the very thought of them made him squirm, and not with the ones who sat with him, for had He not said, "Can the blind lead the blind?" Somehow, he would have to escape the past, the hearties who did not have time, the healthy fresh-faced girls in their sports tunics, with the great bulges on their calves, and those men with flushed faces talking smut in whispers, and guffawing with coarse laughter as though an ape were running his hands over the body of the Madonna.

After the war Eric Miller put the idea of Singapore into his head.

"You know, dear boy," he said, "if you really must teach in this age of the common man, then why not do it in Singapore? They have the reserved sacrament there."

In some ways life in Singapore resembled life in Sydney. Every Sunday he went to the Cathedral Church of St Andrew for the renewal, and it was just like Christ Church, except for the fans, the glare and the clothes of the men and women. The weekly miracle still happened, when the priest turned towards the high altar and in a wavy voice intoned the words:

I be - lie - ve. . . .

The waves of tenderness still gushed out of him, but this time to the English, to the Eurasians, to the Indians, the Chinese, the Malays, even to the one Japanese in the congregation, the sole representative of that people who had tortured some of his fellow-countrymen during the war. Christ, the love of Christ, made him tender with everyone, yes even, as he used to tell me, with his Asian brother.

In some ways, though, I thought Cecil had changed when I met him in Singapore towards the end of 1955. He dressed more ostentatiously, just to show that a Christian could take thought for the body. Anyone, he told me, who felt called to deliver a message could not be a frump as well as a cripple. This desire to proselytize for Christ, he told me, overwhelmed him the first time they sang the Creed in the Singapore Cathedral. As he put it, were not the Asians cripples too? Did they not need a spiritual crutch? As soon as we met in Cecil's flat he began to tell me about the ones he hoped to do something about — not many, mind you, but a beginning, a grain of mustard seed.

"You simply must meet Mary," he said. "No, she hasn't got another name — she's Eurasian. She's awfully pretty, but I do wish she would stop fidgeting with the bangles on her arm. They put all their money into that sort of thing, you know. Strange, isn't it? But as my mother used to say, we've all got to live our own lives. But as I was saying, we must do something about Mary. She got into the wrong hands here — you've no idea, the place is lousy with prots — Singapore's full of them.

And, of course, they only had to tell Mary that Christ was an Asian, and that was that. Now, bless my heart and soul, I hear she's talking to the Romans — not that I've anything against that. Some of my best friends are Roman Catholics. But do you know" — leaning forward on the divan — "Lee tells me — you don't know Lee, but he's another one I must have a word to you about — Lee tells me — no, it's too incredible — I can't believe it. Our Mary, he tells me, is infatuated with Rome because of the name of the Holy Mother of God. But I must tell you about Lee. He's Chinese . . . yes, devilish difficult to find out what's in his mind. But I think he really wants to go to the Cathedral, only he's scared Gupta will tease him about it. But of course, I keep forgetting you haven't met Gupta either. He's the other one who drops in from time to time. I ask him to come here to sort himself out a bit. One day I'll tell him he's a soul in Hell. You know, he says he likes mankind. Not that it stops him sneering at me for belonging to the Swimming Club. But of course you don't know our Swimming Club. . . . Well, when I tell him a club is like a home where you only invite the people like yourself, he snorts and raves, and shrieks at me in that high-pitched voice of his — what tiresome voices these Indians have — yes, shrieks away that if I really believed all that stuff about Christ and loving everyone, then I wouldn't join such a club and insult the millions of Asians who aren't allowed in. Of course they exaggerate, you know. When I told him I had work to do there, that they needed a Christian witness, needed my prayers as much as he did, he snapped back at me — you'll find the Indians drop the mask quicker than the Chinese — 'Anyone can pray,' he said, 'but it takes courage to stand up to the English in Singapore.' "

While Cecil poured this out to me in a mood of what he called a believer's confidence, my eyes kept settling on the statues of Buddha and Siva which flanked a thirteenth-century crucifix on his shelf. Cecil noticed this and commented, "It helps them to see I'm sympathetic."

I did not see him for a few weeks after that. I suppose it was the reference to sympathy which made a return visit seem attractive, for one always assumes that those who crave love and sympathy will understand those who are racked with guilt and damnation. But it is not so.

I sensed almost as soon as I entered Cecil's flat that sultry afternoon that it was not the occasion to discuss doomsday for *orang putih*. He seemed desperately pleased to see me. He introduced me to Mary, who giggled. We shook hands and then she started to fidget with her bangles. Then I shook hands with Lee, who followed the Buddha's advice when he met me and averted the eyes; and then with Gupta who made me suffer, because ... well, there are Indians who can make you feel in a handshake that you are responsible for all the crimes of the white man since that day when he made his first proud boast at Malacca. Gupta was one of them.

But Cecil soon swept such thoughts out of the mind.

"I'm going to put you down next to Mary," he said, "because I think you two would have a lot in common." A remark which started up the giggles in Mary again, and quite febrile fidgets with the bangles. Cecil reached out with one hand for the shelf to steady him while he writhed his body into position with each arm stretched along the polished shelf, looking as though he needed such a crutch, while he took up the threads of the conversation that had been going on before I entered. "I'm glad you decided to drop in, Charles," he said, "because Lee here has been telling us how surprised his brother was to find people in Sydney were nice and friendly to him, and I was about to tell him when you came in there was no problem for me because the love of Christ had made it possible for me to love my Asian brother. . . ."

He looked at Mary, and at Lee and at Gupta tenderly, compassionately — though not without condescension. I noticed his eyes were moist, but that even in a moment of exaltation, a moment of giving himself, the body remained taut. I really think he would have begun to cry, and wanted them to cry too, as though the tears of all of them would symbolize their mystical communion, their passing into a state beyond pain, and ridicule, and hatred, as though Christ had vouchsafed them such a vision that they would not want to hurt and destroy. . . .

Mary cheated him of this moment by a giggling fit, a paroxysm of giggling during which she managed to gasp words out of her shaking body in snatches:

116

"It's — it's the love of Christ — which makes — which makes Cecil like us!"

Lee's face was immobile, and I was far too inexperienced then to read his mind — as though one could find a meaning in a blank sheet. Gupta exulted in silence, because, at such a moment silence was more wounding than speech. Slowly a very pleased smile stole over his face, as it steals over the faces of all such men when the behaviour of their enemies stirs whispers in their minds that theirs is a righteous anger, theirs a righteous hatred.

Within a few weeks Cecil's remark had gone the rounds in Singapore. Students roared with laughter when Gupta retailed it. Up and coming English civil servants dined out on it. An elegant hostess begged, "Do tell us about that priceless remark by the Australian young man."

I wondered then as I wonder now why he of all people should be brought to derision.

A Moment of Illumination

EVER since he could remember, his Ma had warned him to keep out of the way of white folks. "I don't want no boy of mine to be in no trouble," she used to say to him. Up till then he had learned all he knew about life from his mother. When he asked his Ma why he couldn't speak to white children like he spoke to coloured children she put her arm round his shoulders and said, "Son, there jist ain't nothin' you kin do about it." And when he asked her whether it was like the cabins they lived in, and the schools they went to and the churches they attended, like the dogwood and the virginia creeper and the hot sun in summer and the ice on the ponds in winter, something from everlasting, like they sang about in church on Sundays, she said. "Yes, son, I guess it's somethin' like that."

So he grew up in Durham, learning to accept that there were places where he could not go and things he could not be in life. To all his deeper questions his Ma replied, "I don't want no boy of mine to be lynched." So when he asked her, he then being eight, and she a deserted wife of eight years' standing, "Mama, if God loved me, why did he make me black?" she scolded him, but secretly she was so pleased and proud that after church each Sunday she waited till all the respectable women from the six front pews in the Mount Vernon Baptist Church in Durham in the great State of North Carolina were silent, and said, "Did I tell you what my boy said to me last week? . . ."

I can well believe her boy found comfort in the services at this Baptist Church until he was fifteen or sixteen. I say "comfort" because he never bothered to ask himself whether any of the things they talked about and read about and sang about were really true. He had never asked himself if God made the world or if Christ was the son of God. I suspect he recited each week the last words of the creed, ". . . and I look for the resurrection of the dead and the life of the world to come", not as an affirmation of his faith, but rather as a statement of solidarity, of oneness with his own people in the church, because only inside the church did he ever feel a whole and complete person, while everything he experienced outside the church was calculated to make him feel dirty and inferior.

Each week he looked forward to that moment in the service called the "moments of personal fellowship" when he turned to the person on his left and then to the person on his right and embraced them. It was as though for a moment all the hatred in the world he knew, all the cruelty, the savagery, those terrifying "Stand aside, nigger!" — "What are you doing here, boy?" — or those notices, "The management reserves the right to refuse service to any person whatsoever," had disappeared off the face of the earth. An old man, his face bearing the anguish and suffering of his people, stood up in front of the congregation, and, leaning backwards at an angle which suggested that were he not supported by some invisible hand he must fall, shouted in joy: "Yes, man, for forty years I'se been a-leaning on the Lord . . . and he never let me fall, no sirree," while a woman in the choir, gowned and hooded like college students, with a gleam of light shining in her eyes as though her whole body were full of light, with a voice which had that cry of anguish of her people in their long history of darkness and despair, and at the same time that tenderness, that power to touch the heart, as though she had seen all the beauty and the horror in life, and had acquired somewhere, somehow, not only the skill to survive, but the will to endure, began to sing: "Take me to the water now." Then his mother would begin to cry, and though he wished Mama would not do such things when he was sitting next to her, she would begin to call out, "Oh thank you, Jesus, thank you." He would sit there transfigured, carried he knew not where, even believing in the mood of the moment that maybe there was such a water which could wash away that dirt in their lives, and make them all clean. It never occurred to him that some of the dirt in life might never be washed away.

Most of all he loved to listen to the preacher. As a boy he had two heroes — Joe Louis because he was the only coloured man who could knock anyone down; and the pastor because . . . well, it was difficult to put these things in words, but maybe it was because when he listened to the preacher, he suddenly understood everything. He loved it especially when he preached to them about Christ and the fishermen. The preacher would begin by asking the congregation if they liked fishing and they replied, so warm and friendly, "Yes, man, we sure like fishing." Then the preacher told them the story of how one day on the Sea of Galilee the apostles had gone fishing. Just as they might go fishing in the Smoky Mountains: "You like to go a-fishing in the Smokies?" "Yeaman, we like to go fishing in the Smokies." Only this time the apostles caught no fish, until Jesus told them to cast their nets on the other side of the boat, where they caught so many that the nets broke. "Are you listening to me brothers?" "Yes, man, we're a-listening." "Now — the boat, that's the church . . . and the net, that's the gospel of the good news . . . and the sea, that's society, and just as society contains all sorts and conditions. . . . You know, folks, what sort of people there are in human society!" "Yes, man, we sure know that!" "Well, the ocean contains all sorts of fish, sole, codfish, catfish . . . sharks." And as he listened to the words of the preacher it seemed to him that everything slipped into place . . . that just as monsters preyed on the helpless creatures in the mighty deep, so it was the same in his little world in Durham . . . that it had been like this for a long time, and would be so for a long time. So as he sang the hymns with fervour each week after the sermon, again they seemed to explain the pattern in his own life, that badge or stain of inferiority and weakness under which coloured folks had to live all their lives. He sang about his own foulness, of his weakness, of his unworthiness, and, as he sang, it seemed as though he and all of them were singing about the history of their people, as though all the suffering and the humiliation acquired a meaning in that story about some dark deed in the past for which they must be punished to the end of time, and that promise of a happy issue out of their afflictions in the life of the world to come. Then, like his mother, he wanted to say, "Thank you, Jesus, thank you," not as the man who had got beyond mockery and despair, or had said those words of comfort to the woman taken in adultery which replaced the monstrous cruelty of stoning her without the eye of pity (for as yet he knew nothing of that madness). Nor was it because he needed to believe that a time would come when the eyes of the blind would be opened, when the lame would walk and the deaf would hear, and the sea would give up her dead. Those promises touched him not at all. His Jesus had hung on that cross, not lynched like so many of his own people in a cruel, meaningless death. His Jesus had hung there so that all who came after Him might get into Heaven — even the least of His little ones, the coloured people. That was why he could never sing any words about Heaven without a catch in the throat. Sometimes he broke down and sobbed just as he had as a little child when, overwhelmed by all the terror in the world, he had hidden his face deep in his mother's lap. Only now he cried for joy, for the promise of release, for the promise that as one of God's children he too had wings, that he was part of God's plan. So what did it matter if the white boy sang his "*You* in *your* small corner, and I in mine."

What if the students from Duke or Chapel Hill in their insolence, or perhaps not knowing what they were doing, sang those words:

> *Take me back to the land of cotton,*
> *That's where segregation's not forgotten. . . .*

— what did it matter, let them take the coloured man's goods and chattels, and even his life, what were these beside God's promise to all his children? From his mother he had learned how to survive in this world . . . and from the church how to survive till the life of the world to come. In the Mount Vernon Baptist Church he even began to understand something which his mother could never explain, why some were rich and some were poor, why white folks drove in plushy cars while coloured folks travelled in niggermobiles.

After leaving school he studied political science at the North Carolina State College. He began to read Richard Wright and James Baldwin; and by the end of his first year was devouring *Let My People Go*. He read *Ebony* each week in the downtown press stand, but became more and more irritated with C.O.R.E. and N.A.A.D.C.P. He grew a thin-lined moustache on his upper lip, and trained the hairs to stand erect and clipped as on a lady's eyebrow brush. He began to tell his fellow students at North Carolina State College, that the Baptist Church had outlived its usefulness as a crutch for the Negro people — that that crutch must now be slipped away from under their armpits — that they must reap the reward for their labour in this world and not pin their hopes on some old maid's story of a meeting beyond the grave. There was much more about the role of the Baptist Church as a bar to the forward march of his people, always winding up with a fierce, truculent: "I'm telling you, man, religion stinks."

On summer nights he put on his pork-pie hat, which perched at a cocky angle on his head, a sort of battle-cry, or so he liked to think, of the new spirit amongst his people; and walked down West Main with that frozen buttock walk, the head tossed back, the nostrils flared like some thoroughbred rearing for a trial of strength. In the bathroom he had long ago given up singing:

> *Foul I to the fountain fly,*
> *Wash me Saviour or I die.*

Now he sang with cheeky irreverence:

> *'Cause my hair is curly,*
> *'Cause my teeth are pearly,*
> *Just because I always wear a smile,*
> *Like to dress up in the latest style, . . .*
> *That's why they call me shine.*

His mother grieved, and mooned and mooched about the house, and was heard less and less to say, "Did I ever tell you about my boy?" and more and more to sing to herself, in a voice in which she seemed to give expression to all the grief of her people, all their anguish, their humiliations and their sufferings since they left the jungles of Africa and made that journey across the ocean to sweat and labour under the master's lash: "Nobody knows the trouble I've seen, Nobody knows my sorrow."

But he seemed indifferent to the pain he was causing her, quite untouched by all the hopes she had entertained for him as a boy, and only driven on by some passion, some dream of recognition for his people. Gradually he assumed a mocking, taunting note with every person he met. With women he went very quickly to what he called the heart of the matter. "Say, sister," he would begin, "is it to be the songs my mammy taught me . . . or are you going to prove yourself a friend of humanity?" One shy girl at Carolina State College disconcerted him by asking, "What you doing, black boy, with all that hell in your heart?" He ended up by marrying her at Mount Vernon Baptist Church in 1960. It was to be, he said, positively his last appearance as a knee-bender. Next year he began to teach in a Durham secondary school for coloured girls and boys.

For a while they were very happy. He gave her most of what he earned as a teacher, as well as what tenderness he had left after twenty odd years of averting the eyes and pursuing a survivor's morality in a southern State. As for her, in her simple loving kindness, she took the wedding service to mean what it said: she had given him all she had until death did them part.

Soon after a child was born the trouble started. When the child cried she wanted to slap it, not severely, no more than a tap, as she put it, to get rid of the old Adam inside him. But he winced — because, for him, all force, whether the six-shooter white folks wore on their hips or the harness leather they used to whip black boys, or the mildest lightest tap of the hand, reminded him of what white folks did to his people. So he chided her, at first gently, as one of them white folks. Later, as the screamings became louder, and the beatings more drawn out, she used a piece of leather from an old trace harness she had picked up for free in one of the deserted stables on the outskirts of Durham, which he, with his rather lurid imagination, called the white man's whip. Soon he found relief from such scenes and arguments in the local pool-room where coloured folks played ball, drank wood liquor and swapped yarns about wives and girls, on the assumption that women had only one precious gift for a man, in return for which they tormented him for all his weaknesses. When he touched on his own difficulties, speaking in riddles as sensitive men will, the older men laughed bitterly. "Man, I tell you," one said, "all women are fiends." And, when he hinted rather obliquely at terrible scenes after night-fall in their wooden cabin, the very shame of betrayal stilled his tongue. For in the early days there had been moments of great happiness, moments when he knew what the preacher meant when he said those words, "The peace of God which passeth all understanding." So it was only gradually that he found he could enjoy without a pang the savagery of the pool-room. "Man," an old man told him, "they want the lot." But such explanations did not touch him deeply, because, though good for a laugh, they were not part of that great drama which the white men and black men were playing with America as their stage and the civilized world as their audience.

So it came as a shock to discover just how deeply he had become involved in these fights with his wife about the control of their child. Within a year or so the differences had spread over every aspect of their lives. They quarrelled over what the child should eat, what he should wear, and how he should spend his leisure. She favoured the TV, he was keen on meccano. And the more he withdrew from their life together, the more he sought refuge and relief in the pool-room, the more she turned on him with that look, not of hatred, or rancour or animosity, but of total disapproval, so that in moments of drunkenness, which also were becoming more and more frequent, having started as occasional Saturday night carousals and drifted into an indispensable drug to enable him to "face reality", he played with the idea that all their wives had sold their souls to the white devils on the top of the hill — only to reject his thought the next day as soon as a white man shouted at him: "Boy, get moving." Then he knew again, even if for one drunken moment he had been mad enough to forget it, who was really in charge in white America.

Still, the home rows stretched on so that his wife's criticism ranged wider and wider, and pried deeper and deeper into his wounds and his guilt till at length it seemed to him when they confronted each other over some trivia — the non-payment of a bill, the quality of the coffee, or the number of blankets on the bed — that either the voice must be stilled or he would go mad. It was during one of these rows that he first struck her with his fist, not so much to hurt her as for the sake of the peace that would descend when her voice could no longer be heard and her eyes could no longer mock him. To his dismay he found this last state worse than the first, for after the blow, in addition to the pain he had endured from her intruding into the very heart of him, he had to endure the remorse for an impulsive sock on the jaw. Then he began to resent her not only as his tormentor, the "fiend" in the language of the pool-room, but as the cause of his remorse which nothing, neither drink, nor the companionship of men, not good deeds, nor buying presents for the kid, could silence. To his dismay he found that the more he sought to quieten that little voice inside him, the louder and louder the voice became, not only undrownable by buckets of bourbon, but insisting on more savagery towards the wife, and insisting that unless she were crushed and trampled on it would go on talking louder and louder and louder. So, whipped on by the bayings and shoutings of that voice, he rushed out of the pool-room, down the unlit unpaved street, and up the weevil-eaten steps of his cabin, shouting that he would flog the daylights out of her . . . only to find, after he had battered down the front door, that his wife had fled, leaving his child cowering on a bed in a dark corner in the front room, whom in his rage he began to belabour with his belt, shouting blasphemies and obscenities, while the child, the whites of his eyes themselves betraying both the pain and the terror, shrieked and begged him, please Daddy, not to hit him no more — till the police arrived and led him away and placed him in the lock-up from where he could see, through his barred window, the monument to the boys who wore grey in 1861-5.

There he prepared to "face the music" in the Recorder's Court, knowing from the folk-lore of his people not only that no Negro could expect justice, let alone understanding, from a white man, but knowing too the hurts and humiliations to which a coloured man was exposed when the Recorder said the ominous words, "Tell us your story." He knew too that other difference between justice for the white man and the coloured man, that after the coloured man had confessed to the crime of drunkenness the court recorder sent him for eighty days' hard labour on the roads, while the white man paid his fine and tasted his first bourbon within half an hour of the trial. Besides it was well known that the Recorder's Court was a sort of social scientist's laboratory for those northerners and British who were sniffing round for indecency in the south like dogs round a bitch in the streets. And he wondered how he could endure that.

So it came as a surprise to him when the Recorder asked him in a voice which suggested some sympathy, "Tell us your story." And though there were interruptions at which the white men in the room sniggered and nudged each other — "Tell me, boy, did you cut that girl?" — he could say truthfully and with pride, "No, sir, I didn't cut her" . . . and became so confused that he added, "I was too goddam drunk to remember what I did." But of course, she did, she remembered everything; women always do. She responded quickly when the Recorder told her to get up into the box and tell her story. She described how the first thing she heard was him banging on the door, and swearing, so that she asked, polite like — though, if your Honour pleases, she was terrible scared at the time — "What do you want?" Then she stopped and flushed and said he had replied with a rudeness; and when the Recorder pressed her to say what it was, she, blushing the while, and dropping her eyes in what to him was a mockery of shame, said: "Well, your Honour, he said '. . . only kiss my arse and I'll let you go free.' " Then the Recorder asked him whether he wanted to be free in that way, and when he said, yes he did, not believing that he ever could, the Recorder said something which he would not have believed if he had not heard it himself. The Recorder told the whole court: "I believe it is my duty to keep this man away from this woman."

And then it happened, that moment of illumination, when he realized that in the world there were not just problems for coloured folks, but problems for men, that on this he had a bond with the Recorder deeper than the bond of colour, just as on other questions, such as death, he had a bond with all men, including his wife. So when the Recorder asked him, if he, the Recorder, helped him to keep away from her, would he pay a fine, he began to cry, and he said yes, he would pay the fine, and as he walked out of the court he lifted his eyes to the Recorder man to man, and he remembered how it had been said of old that a people that had walked in darkness would one day see a great light.

A Long Time Ago

THE YEAR Charles Hogan turned thirteen his mother sent him to Barrabool for the holidays — "It will help to make a man of you," she said. So one Monday in January 1926 after one of those painful farewells in which his mother kept asking that unanswerable question — "Are you sure you'll be all right, Charles dear?" — Hogan set out in the slow train which rocked slowly over the dry, stoney plains between Melbourne and Geelong; it stopped there for refreshments and then crawled off again over flat grey lands towards Ballarat. At Barrabool Hogan was met by his cousin, Evan, a gawk of fourteen without a brain in his head, as Hogan's father used to put it, and with shifty eyes which evaded all contact with other eyes and only stayed still when looking at the ground. But still he was capable of dumb devotion to anyone who left him alone.

There were also Tom and Nellie, the faithful retainers who had been born on Barrabool Station in the days when Hogan's great-grandfather sold meat and vegetables to the gold diggers on their way from Geelong to Ballarat; the old couple had lived on into an age where they were strangers. With Tom at the reins, Hogan perched beside him, and Nellie and Evan in the rear, they set out for the home station with Tom muttering from time to time that "Things were different in your great-grandfather's time" as the fence posts swished past to the measured trot of the horse and a lark hovered overhead, and sang, as though pitting its beauty against sun and sky, and wind and rain, and all that men could do. Hogan began to feel a peace settle inside him.

After an hour, to the shouts of "Whoa back, Tiny, whoa back" from Tom, the jinker halted in a cloud of dust. Evan jumped down to open the gate into the drive along which they travelled till they came to another gate, after which the road changed from dust and gravel to clean polished pebbles, skirted on both sides by trim lawns, with flowering shrubs and great tall trees overspreading the driveway. The horse raised its head, dogs barked, and tugged at their chains, parrots dipped from tree to tree, while overhead through the inter-twining branches crows kept watch beneath the vast blue dome of the sky, squawking for dead flesh. Soon they swept out into the open where terraced lawns and croquet courts, and statues of classical figures, draped with vine-leaves, faded off into the horizon; and on the other side stood a blue stone house, skirted on the front by an iron roofed veranda with Paul Scarlett roses blooming in profusion on its pillars, and a Bougainvillea creeper hanging wantonly over the guttering.

Miss Isabel, Charles's great-aunt, and her lady companion were waiting for them on the veranda. Miss Isabel greeted Charles with a brush of her cheek against his cheek, and a "You're becoming more like your father every day, but I don't suppose you can help that." Then they walked through the halls where ancestors peered down, their faces as inscrutable as all the members of his mother's family, through the library, the drawing-room, the sitting-room and the dining-room from which a corridor branched off into the sleeping quarters. Miss Isabel led Charles into his own room where the whitewashed basin, the snow-white linen on the bed, the whitewash on the walls, contrasted with the dark cedar frame of the bed, the cedar chest of drawers, and the dark flooring boards.

There was a curious order and serenity in the house. Bed clothes were never out of place, the books were arranged in orderly rows, voices were never raised. There were no shouts, no tears, no laughter: there were bells to summon you for meals, and grace before meat. Charles very quickly slipped into the routine of the house. He rose with the breakfast bell, helped himself from the sideboard, listened to the talk about his mother's family and the olden days, and then at the end of the meal went down on his knees at the side of the chair, and enunciated clearly when Miss Isabel, her eyes closed, said: "Let us all say after me the words Our Saviour taught us to say — 'Our Father which art in Heaven . . .'"

Then they rose, and went about their own business. Charles and Evan fished for blackfish in the nearby creek. When they were sick of that, Evan shinned up gum-trees to look for cockatoo eggs in the hollow left where a branch had snapped off at the trunk, while the mother bird screeched and squawked and pecked, with her yellow crest quivering; and Charles, timid as ever, stood at the foot of the tree, hurling yonnies at the cocky, or beating the tree with a stick to frighten the mother bird away. At other times they rode out mustering, or sat yarning on the sliprails while one of the stationhands dagged and tarred the sheep.

Towards evening they took a rifle each from the armoury, and slid on their stomachs through the tall grass in the orchard to stalk the rabbits which, if undisturbed, came out at dusk to nibble grass and jump for apples in the lower boughs. Miss Isabel had offered a prize to the first one to hit a rabbit on the jump.

At nightfall they returned to the homestead, where they tubbed, and changed into clean linen, and supped off cold meats and salads, and bread and jam and cream, and tea served in cups fit for a man to drink, after which Miss Isabel said during the hush at the end of the meal: "Let's say again after me the words He taught us to use." And down they went on their knees beside their chairs, Miss Isabel, the lady companion, Miss Jury, Evan and Charles, and it was as though the Amen was a way of saying "Yes" to all the wonders and glories of the day, till Evan said to Charles as they were moving to the drawing-room, "You wait till Sunday."

But, for the moment, Charles for once was not apprehensive: sufficient unto the day was the pleasure thereof, he told himself, and savoured his own joke, while the lady companion arranged the cards for her evening game of huff patience with Miss Isabel. Every time the lady companion made a move, Miss Isabel wheezed, "Goodness, how stupid of you, Miss Jury." and, in between her own masterly moves, while the lady companion was working out her next one, she turned to Charles and said, "When your great-grandfather was chairman of the Legislative Council in Melbourne, people said it was the first time a doctor, a gentleman, and a statesman had held the billet."

While Miss Jury pondered over her next move, and whispered, "Oh, dear, I fear I'm going to do something stupid again," Miss Isabel turned again to Charles and said, "Did I ever tell you about the death of your great uncle George . . . hit his head, you know, on the stable rafter when he was returning from the harvest thanksgiving service in Barrabool. Your great aunt Agnes never got over it, you know . . . she moped about the old house, and turned it into a funeral parlour."

Then, with a triumphant "Huff" from Miss Isabel, and an "Oh dear, how stupid of me" from Miss Jury, the game ended. Miss Isabel walked over to the harp, moved up and down the scale, paused, and then started a golden melody which flooded the room — Charles was puzzled. The words, he knew, were banal, yet the music touched him as never before, as though it were throwing light on some dark side of human life, and giving him strength to face it. It was that old hymn "Take it to the Lord in prayer." It was Saturday evening, and after they lit their candles, and brushed cheek against cheek for goodnight, Miss Isabel said, "Tomorrow is the Lord's day. Let us do what He would have wanted us to do." And Charles wanted to ask, "What was that?" but decided that perhaps he had better not, as he did not want Miss Isabel to tell his mother that, although they had all liked him very much, it was a pity he was so cheeky and common like his father.

The next morning the blinds were drawn in the house, the

curtains in full sail, and darkness where before there had been light. When they went down on their knees after breakfast Miss Isabel apologized to the Lord for all of them because they had sinned against Him in thought, word, and deed, and there was no health in any of them.

After prayers Charles and Evan mooched and mooned around the house at a loss how to do nothing without being bored. At lunch, which was frugal, with none of the creams, the home-made jams, the pies, and the fruit salads of week days, there were more prayers than before, more grovellings, and, more apologies for past faults, and promises of amendment for the future. This time all the servants were invited to join in the prayers. Tom and Nellie shuffled into the room — so did the cook, the parlour-maid, and the pantry-maid, and the rouse-about, and the yardman.

At the end of the prayers Miss Isabel asked them all to join her in the drawing-room in the singing of a hymn. The servants protested their unworthiness to join in such company, but Miss Isabel majestically led the way and they followed. After they had all gathered round the harp, she plucked the string and turned to Tom and said, "Now, Tom, you choose. . . ."

"Please, Miss Isabel, I would like 'Take it to the Lord in prayer'."

But this time the music failed to cast its magic spell over Charles. The words were too painful. What was this "it" which you were supposed to take to the Lord in prayer? It could not be requests for things you wanted, because if so, this Lord was a great fraud. Nor could it have anything to do with requests that the strong should cease to torment the weak, because there too, the Lord, Charles had found, was the greatest letter-down of all time. Yet here they were, Miss Isabel, Tom, Nellie, the cooks, the servants, the rouseabouts, singing those words:

> *Oh what peace we often forfeit,*
> *Oh what needless pain we bear —*
> *Can we find a friend so faithful?*
> *Who did all our sorrows share?*
> *Do thy friends despise, forsake, thee?*
> *Take it to the Lord in prayer.*

Charles wanted the hymn to end. Yet, as he looked round

the room, he was aware that the others did not share his impatience, or his anger. Every time they sang the line "Take it to the Lord in prayer" a wave of beauty passed over Miss Isabel's face. As the last note of the Amen died away, and a reverential hush descended on the little group, Miss Isabel smiled at Tom, and then turned towards the others with such tenderness in her eyes, that Charles believed he saw tears bathe her cheeks. Tom too stood there, as one refreshed, while the tears rolled down his cheeks. Charles's anger evaporated: he wondered why this hymn, with its banal words and its simple melody, could move a group of adults to tears. The next night he was back at his boarding-school . . . where in a few days he had drifted back into his old cynicism towards those people who promised to comfort and relieve him according to his several necessities.

At the Exhibition

WHEN Margot and Chester arrived at the opening of an exhibition of paintings in Canberra under the patronage of the British Council everyone in the gallery looked at her. The hair, which was modelled on a dignified compromise between the bee-hive and curly cut, rose gracefully from her brow. The eyebrows had been plucked and cropped into a clean-cut line; the eyelashes had been tinged to a deeper black than nature had provided. This heightened the effect nature had begun, the effect not so much of a painted but rather of a waxed doll with wasps feeding on her heart.

I had walked into the exhibition just behind Margot, and had some idea of what sort of a day it was for her. Chester was like a stage manager for a prima donna: he provided the properties, the Jaguar Mark IV, the exotic drinks, the expensive presents and the beautifully tailored clothes for Margot's public appearances. On this occasion I only heard snatches of their conversation as they walked up the stairs. When Chester said that in more ways than one it had been a trying day, Margot drawled that she had been far too busy to notice it. When he risked inviting her to join him later at dinner, she sighed the sigh of the bored, and said that as she was free that night she might as well, but he must promise not to take her to one of those ghastly petty-bourgeois homes in Canberra where the peasant bureaucrats ate their ghastly tea at the impossible hour of six-thirty. To which challenge, while Margot made her final preparations for her entry into the exhibition, Chester responded with a promise to rise to the occasion.

This was superb. She lowered her eyes when the eyes of the people in the gallery swung on to her. Even the Archbishop was startled for a moment, till he remembered the advice of the lord Buddha — more efficacious, he had found, for the women of snares and nets than the standards of purity demanded by the founder of his own religion — and averted the eyes.

Margot always emitted a promise of voluptuousness, while planting in men's minds the terror or threat that to take her successfully was a feat reserved for the gods. As though to underline her power to cause uproar in the trousers of all men, while being takable by none, she had perfected the art of leaning forward ever so slightly towards men in conversation so that their eyes could see what their hands could not touch.

Two waiters converged on Margot with trays of drinks. She smiled gaily, chose a martini for herself from one tray and a sherry for Chester from the other. One of the lecturers from the University, his academic detachment sadly shaken by the suggestive partition visible as the dress curved down and up, rushed up to her and fumbled for a suitable compliment. While the words wrestled with desire, Margot, who was as astute as the most skilful preferment climber in Canberra in sensing who were the lightweights and who the heavyweights in any gathering, did not wait for the compliment.

Just before she had entered, an English literary agent who had been some years in Australia, Cecil Cripps, was telling a rather earnest Fullbright scholar that the question he had asked — "Who are the successors to the angry young men?" — was, of course, the question of the day in England, and of course, a most tricky one to answer. I might have believed Cripps had a genuine interest in literature and art if I had not seen him break off so many conversations to serve interests closer to his heart. He had risked a carnation in his buttonhole for the occasion and was giving off his usual odour of decay, for the grubby cuffs of his shirts, the pouches below the eyes, the faint stalactites of flesh hanging from his double chin, gave off a musty odour. I might have been impressed by the reverend and indeed enthusiastic way he talked about art and learning as he circulated amongst guests at the opening of exhibitions, if I had not heard him dine out later on, in the camp of the Philistines, where over coffee, cigars and brandy, he mimicked our poets and painters with such brilliance that one of the generals present damaged one of his war wounds from laughing, and the wife of an ambassador from a country with whom Australia enjoys the closest possible friendship asked his permission to put his stories on tape.

Cripps bounded up to Margot, and held her hand for a time which Chester found quite unnecessarily prolonged, and told her she had come as usual at a "singularly felicitous" moment, as he was just looking for someone who had what one did not find very often in this country, someone with the "infectious friendliness of the Orstralians" (one of Cripps's skills with the voice was to insinuate the idea of a horse when he pronounced the word Australian) "and something more than a smattering of knowledge of the culture of the old world, to show Thistlethwaite around the show. And, who is better qualified, and, dare I add, more lovely than you for such a chore?"

Margot demonstrated her pleasure by squeezing his hand just enough to convey thanks without issuing an invitation. Stories of the literary gamesmanship of Thistlethwaite had become regular currency for the mockers for the past ten years or so. It was said he was fond of quoting Goethe's remark that when Byron reflected, he was like a little child. There was a story, too, of one young writer who had taken to his bed for a week after Thistlethwaite had blasted his first avant-garde poem in a review in *Encounter*. It was even said, although this may be quite an apocryphal version, that the young man, with that curious drive of the vulnerable to expose themselves before their tormentors, rashly asked Thistlethwaite what he really thought of his poetry, and when Thistlethwaite, sniffing as though there were a nasty smell in the place, snorted, "No one told me, dear boy, that you wrote poetry," the young man went out and wept bitterly. The mockers greatly enjoyed that monumental piece of rudeness, because, as they saw it, it showed Thistlethwaite as a true defender of standards in an age of mediocrity.

I had had some sympathy with the wife of Thistlethwaite ever since I had been told that she was capable of saying quietly to the men who were bemoaning their cruel fate to be born into a society where their works were judged by the same market value as a pound of butter, "Have you ever thought of what it is like for a woman who is not properly married?"

As soon as Cripps introduced Margot, Chester and me to Thistlethwaite and his wife one could see her long-drawn-out agony which had prompted such a remark, for Thistlethwaite began by gently flattering Margot.

"You're the young woman," he said to her, "who is brave enough to explain these pictures to me." And I could see at once the pleasure on his face when she responded to his flattery. I mean, he was a man who enjoyed it when the weaknesses of other people caused the jaws of the trap he had set to snap on them. While Margot began to fall into this trap to expose herself, Thistlethwaite led her off to see the pictures, while Chester, Thistlethwaite's wife and I followed behind, preserving that uneasy silence which descends on the cast-offs as they bring up the rear in the procession of a celebrity.

We stopped in front of the first picture, which set so many traps for the unwary that even Margot played safe, allowing a scarcely audible "mmm" to escape from her mouth, and a puzzled look to form in her eye. But Thistlethwaite came to her rescue by remarking that it was difficult for him to make anything of the paintings so long as his eyes were so delighted by the dress Margot was wearing. To which Margot replied by clutching her catalogue tightly, and saying with animation that in this country where the men had the taste of pygmies from their dreary devotion to the Welfare State — where the vision did not rise above the aim of a refrigerator in every bungalow — it was quite refreshing to meet a man with an eye for distinction in dress. When Thistlethwaite looked at her as though she were a woman with the intelligence to peer into the very heart of things, Margot was encouraged to risk the generalization that the Welfare State was for provincials, while she herself was only at home with the metropolitans. To which Thistlethwaite replied that Margot seemed to have the poet's vision of life. She reminded him, he said, of an eagle in a sky full of starlings and sparrows and, with a meaningful look towards the senior academics and public servants present, "tom-tits".

This encouraged Margot to use the whisper of intimacy, and the sign language of communion between choice spirits. "You help a woman to become aware of herself." And Thistlethwaite bared his teeth as the jaws of the trap bit more deeply into her soul. The colonials were giving him a field day.

I was hoping Chester and Mrs Thistlethwaite did not hear this exchange, though I knew that the thought of Chester hearing it was something which would give an added edge to Margot's pleasure. I wanted also to make some gesture towards Mrs Thistlethwaite, perhaps to touch her elbow gently to show that at least someone in the room pitied her for all humiliations she had suffered, but a glance at her face showed me not so much that she had passed beyond pity, as that she had gathered the strength to endure without putting statues of the Buddha in her room, or taking up yoga, or reading the book of Ecclesiastes.

The curious thing was that at that time I felt no pity for Margot. By the time we reached the fifth or sixth picture (I forget the number but remember the subject, which was "The Revellers") Margot boldly took up Thistlethwaite's challenging: "Well, what about that one?" (By looking very hard I had managed to detect the outlines of four men in evening dress sitting round a table at a night-club.)

"It's George Herbert's point about debauchery," Margot said. "Isn't there a line about the fly that feeds on dung must be stained?"

"Ah," said Thistlethwaite, "once again I see the poet in you is struggling to come to the surface"; and he quoted:

> *Make not thy sport, abuses: for the fly*
> *That feeds on dung, is coloured thereby.*

There was silence between them after that; though, during the pauses between pictures, they communed with each other through the eyes. At the last picture, when Chester rather boldly broke the silence with some inane and brittle clichés, Thistlethwaite, looking very wise, dropped the remark that it was not only the painter and the poet who illuminated the human situation. . . .

I thought we were all in for an evening by candlelight during which Thistlethwaite would discourse on the burden of the mystery, Margot would look decorative and approving, while poor Chester used his best logic-chopping devices in a desperate throw to win the battle for Margot. But such was not to be. When an aide from Government House whispered into Thistlethwaite's ear, he followed him like a lamb.

Margot, in the full flush of her success, called for a celebration, and told us what a wonderfully stimulating and exciting man Thistlethwaite was, and how he had stirred up that thirst for old civilization which nothing in Australia could quench. So I suggested dinner at University House as a compromise, adding that I was sure she had learned to settle for half in Australia. She agreed.

She was just as magnificent at the high table as at the gallery. As a tribute to her creation — I remember in particular how the flower of her corsage set off the black dress, and the white curve of her bosom — everyone insisted that she should sit opposite the Master during dinner. After the sherry, the dry riesling, which we sipped with the fish, and a rich claret which we took with the steak, I was so carried away that I proposed a toast to all pretty women. Margot murmured tenderly, "Dear Charles: is the pain coming back?" and leaned towards me so that I had to avert my eyes. I remembered that once before — when the wine and the food and the sight of Margot gave me the idea that perhaps He would come again, and talk as He had talked by the waters of Galilee before He met the lawyers, and the academics — I had told Margot about my private ache. But my private terror of exposure was quickly lost in the brilliance of the evening. Over the coffee Margot asked me to come to Chester's room where a few choice spirits were gathering to sample a new Madeira which Chester had rather cleverly found in Sydney. I wondered whether anyone was ever alone with Margot, whether the drive for adoration was stronger than the drive for affection.

Chester's room was just as much a display as Margot's creation. A thin shaft of light from a torpedo lamp shone on a rare south Indian carving of the suffering Buddha, a print of Arthur Boyd's "The Mockers" hung over the fire-place, while various trinkets from Borobudur and Angkor were lying on the top of the bookshelves. Out of the silence Margot said rather wistfully, "If one *really* wanted to cease to be a provincial one should live in Rome."

Chester chipped in waspishly, "That's singular, because old spiritual-values Thistlethwaite once wrote a poem which made the point that it was the mark of a second-rate to be pre-occupied with the difference between the provincial and the metropolitan. . . ."

Somewhat to my surprise I saw a globule of a tear roll slowly out of Margot's left eye, and down her cheek. I remembered the remark of the Buddha that he who was free from desire could endure pain and suffering as the lotus leaf bears the rain-drops without blemish. But how could one explain *that* to Margot?

Still Hope for God

I AM STILL not quite sure what it was that drew me to him. I remember thinking, as I sat at the table of that street cafe in Warsaw watching the never-ending flow of people pass by, that there was a man who was not like the English tourists, who either joked when confronted with all that was painful in the human situation or asked me whether I would care to add a note of Australian virility to the conversation. I remember, too, thinking as I looked at him that perhaps here was a man who might be able to explain much that was a mystery to me in this city; why, for example, two neighbouring streets were named "New World Street" and "Resurrection Street". I remember even thinking that perhaps he was the man on whom I might risk that question about pity and tenderness, whether he thought that here in Poland there was a people's democracy which had also preserved the image of Christ. And I wanted to ask someone who was interested in what it all had been for, whether here in Poland the human miracle might occur, and that after the people had got their labour-savers and their pill, their lives would not become empty and stupid — yes, and boring and sad.

So when he asked, shyly and indeed with such diffidence that I promptly avoided his eyes, whether it was "Mozhno" to join me at my table, I said it would be a great pleasure for me; and, after trying each other in English and German, we decided we could at least communicate something to each other in English — if I promised to keep off those Aussie words I love to use when speaking about those things which move me more than it suits a man to say. And I liked, too, the tone of his remarks in the opening exchanges before we had settled on our subject for the day; he could joke without being frivolous, or cynical, and, at the same time, he could avoid those boring lectures which the humourless intellectuals here, complete with their huge sunglasses, seemed called on to deliver to visitors from the west. A tourist easily becomes the prey of the local bores, or misfits, or the lame who clutch a stranger because maybe he could do what no one else in life could ever do — get them over the stile. So I liked it when he told me with a twinkle in his eye, which I caught, but did not linger on, that in Poland people say you should not be too critical of the Government unless you want to become a long-term tourist in Russia.

It was while we were laughing over that that I decided to risk a more general remark. "You think then that there is more freedom in Poland than in Russia?" To which he answered almost with pride, "But of course."

So I asked him to permit me to say to him something which might cause him some pain, though I hoped it would not. And he said, "Please do; and if," he added with a flourish, "I know the answer, it will be my duty as well as my pleasure to tell you." So I asked why it was that if there were fewer spiritual bullies and conformists in Poland (we had trouble over those words) there had nevertheless been such terrible cruelty and bestiality between man and man in Poland at the end of the war. "You know," he said, "when the Russian Army encircled Warsaw, the Polish resistance movement rose to expel the Germans, but the Russians would not so much as lift one little finger to help them. So the Hitlerians systematically butchered those heroes of Warsaw."

I told him that was one example of human evil, hoping, I suppose, that he would catch on to the drift of my mind. . . . "No, Mister Charles Hogan, that was not evil," he said, "that was politics. The Russians thought it was capitalists fighting capitalists, and hoped they would both destroy each other" . . . adding, "Maybe it's not pleasant, but, how do you say it in English, my friend, such is life."

Maybe it was because I looked so dejected after this remark that he added tenderly, his eyes seeming to moisten a little, "But if you want to see the memorial to great human evil in Warsaw, then you must see the memorial to the Jews in the ghetto. . . . Yes, my friend, that is what you must see."

I wondered whether the time had come to ask him, diffidently and, of course, with apologies for seeming to intrude, whether like all sentimental people the Poles were cruel and treacherous — but decided I couldn't because I already knew that vulnerable face would haunt me for days, so why add to his and my pain? But, somewhat to my surprise, he almost anticipated me. "You are wondering," he asked gently, "why such terrible things could happen in Poland?" . . . but, before I could even manage a yes, he had begun to answer his own question in his own way. . . . "That, my friend, is a long story, and we must talk about it on our way to the memorial."

We met again the next afternoon over coffee and ice-creams at the bar of the European Hotel, and then set out to walk through the hot dusty streets to the memorial. On the way we talked about many things. He explained to me that in Warsaw no one had any money, but that they were happy. In the West, he said, people were wealthy, everyone had a car, everyone had a house, how do you say it, Christ has been brought back into Christmas, and we laughed gently over this; everyone has free choice. "Is Christ," he asked with a twinkle, "the symbol of free choice? Yet, my friend, in the West you are not happy, and I will tell you why, my friend . . . there are things in life people prefer to free choice . . . things like the absence of the ghetto murder. Is that not better," he asked, "than to be able to choose between thirty-six flavours of doughnuts?"

And when I asked him whether all being poor together was the price they might have to pay to make sure it did not happen again — asking him this, not to score, or cause him pain, but because it seemed then that a perpetual greyness may be the price we will all have to pay when we stop tormenting each other — he was not too happy about that, and stopped in the street, and took me by the arm, and said, "Here, my friend, you must understand things are getting better all the time."

"But still, you do not get a passport to go to Paris."

"You are right, my friend. There are no passports for Polish people because, my friend, our government thinks Paris is like a beautiful woman — full of snares and nets. We must pray for our Government, my friend."

By then he had stopped again in front of some writing on the street wall.

"Now," he said, "I will translate it for you. Here on 11 December 1943, it says, the Hitlerians shot one hundred of my people. No . . . it is not nice, my friend . . . it is not nice."

We were silent for a time after that until I said, "You know, you Poles remind me of the Irish . . . You have both suffered terribly from an imperialist power. You have both preserved the Church . . . you have some of that tenderness, some of that pity of people who have known terrible humiliations, and cruelty, and swinishness . . . and, yes, in your ceremonial, your exaggerated gestures, your bowings, your scrapings, your kissing the hands of women . . . there is something pathetic in this, something mocking, too, as though you had been so hurt by life, so humiliated, that you were driven to mock at the source of life itself, at women."

"Maybe you are right, my friend, but, you see, for us it is different. Ceremony, my friend, this kissing of the hand, that was the product of one type of society. It is, how shall I express it, a charming remnant of the days of chivalry, and will disappear when the last remnants of feudal and bourgeois society in Poland have been rooted out."

By then we were coming close to the monument and by one of those absurdities in human behaviour I had chosen that moment to tell a story about how some people kill snakes in Australia with a whip, so that we came alongside the monument just as I was explaining how to crack their heads off. Some human situations can only be made bearable by a boorish buffoonery, or so I have found. So there we were, having to change our mood from the hunter's world perhaps to the idea that this particular act of human swinishness was one of the death throes of a decaying social order. And as I looked, or gaped at those stone figures under that hot sun, the one thought that kept recurring was that only poetry or music could illuminate such a moment in the long-drawn-out human drama of good and evil.

All I could see was a man with the head bowed in a grief for which this piece of stone seemed so inadequate. Anyhow, what could these men of the brave new world tell us about the secrets of the human heart, when they so shamelessly boasted of their indifference to the sentiments of pity and terror? Another man was reaching for the dagger of revenge, but what use was it to kill such monsters? And another seemed to be striving for a better future, though I could not tell from his face what that future was going to be like. It all seemed terribly inadequate to the purpose.

I was thinking of turning to my friend and saying with some firmness, "Look, I could understand if the sculptor had said, 'I'm going to show that the imagination of man's heart was evil from the start', because that at least would be telling us something; but this tells me nothing about either God or man." But it was just as well I had not begun to speak about those things, because the monument had evoked quite different thoughts in the mind of my friend. "I will tell you something, my friend," he said, putting his arm around me, "the Jewish people . . . they were always good at making money, and the Polish people . . . they were always bad at making money. We Poles are not money-grubbers, my friend." And he shrugged his shoulders. We began to walk away from the monument, I a pace or two apart, as though to communicate that a bond had snapped, but he went on, not sensing my dismay: "And now, there are no Jewish people and so now there is no problem, my friend," adding with a mirthless hollow laugh that contained a plea for understanding and sympathy, "but still the Polish people are very poor. . . . How do you say it in English, my friend. . . . Such is life."

And I suppose I must have begun to look sad, because he

asked me, quite anxiously, and indeed almost with alarm, whether something had upset me, and I wanted to ask him there and then whether he could remember that remark by the Jewish writer Franz Kafka that there was hope for man, but not for God; and if he could remember, I wanted to add sharply that I was thinking how there might be hope for God, but no hope for man. But I knew I could never say this to him, not just because of his kindness to me but because to do it with the authority which the occasion demanded it would be necessary to look straight at him, and that was precisely what I had not been able to bring myself to do ever since he had told me, in one of those rushes of confidence during our first exchange over the coffee and the ices, that the Hitlerians had shot away his left arm.

A Footnote to the Kokoda Story

IN the spring of 1972 the two of us were squatting in the shade at the side of the Kokoda trail. We liked to think of ourselves as special observers of the human scene. He was a poet, a lyric poet with metaphysical longings, and I was a historian who wanted history to say more than most people wanted it to say. After a while the poet said I only became a person when I looked sad. He asked me what was ailing me, you old knight at arms — prithee so sad and wan, fond lover. I said I was considering why there had ever been such horror in a place of beauty — I mean why, for example, did the butterfly have to see such vileness. I could not understand why men had turned one of the beauties of God's creation into a setting for their beastliness and their evil.

Dave told me poets could not tell what it was like to be there. But surely, I said, a low comedian could make vulgar jokes about the men who were there to escape from their wives — "Why not start with some comic irony — about those who were there to get away from their wives, or their girlfriends, or their mothers, or their masters, or some frightful bully of a teacher, and found life at Kokoda was not like an Australian bar, where a man could participate in the one communion service we Australians all believe in. Just think of those tender Aussie eyes meeting over a glass of beer just as a Jap. sniper picked off a drinker at the great communion rail. Or take an even more bizarre scene. Any man perched in a tree on the Kokoda trail knew quite well that if he had a shit the smell of it might give him away and some Jap. sniper would drop him. Artistic, isn't it? Perhaps that is something for the historians: I can imagine an examination question, "Was the main cause of death on the Kokoda trail the inability of Australian snipers to control their bowel actions? Discuss. Give reasons for your answer."

"Yes", I said, "and then there were the ones who were rattled by the snipers. I knew one young soldier who had fought through the whole campaign in North Africa, had roared so drunkenly around Jerusalem shouting he was so hungry he could eat Christ's shin-bones, and shoved lighted cigarettes up the bums of Negro gigolos, and roared with laughter, and went out into the street and lay on his back to vomit into the air so that it dropped down all over his face, and yet did not care a damn — he'd got past caring. Kokoda shook him. His teeth began to chatter. He was so ashamed: he tried to make a joke of it. So he asked his mate whether he was feeling the cold. Well, he survived. But six years later the Chinese got him in Korea. That might be worth a footnote in any story about the battle of the Kokoda trail. They say those who look for salvation in the muck make the best crusaders for Christian civilization. I loved him. I still think of him as one of Kokoda's victims."

Then Dave said he wanted to write a poem about the fuzzy-wuzzies, not about their heroism and all that crap. He wanted to write a savage poem about our young intellectuals from Sydney and Melbourne and Canberra who have made the important discovery that if they called a native "mate", that gave "Whitey" the right to sit on his bum all day while the coloured men did the "hard yakker", as though there were some sort of moral superiority in this life of living off the labour of others. He would start with the historians, the political scientists, the economists, all the secular humanists performing their acts of compassion — the hospital cheerfulness smile at the man cutting the grass, the wave of the hand intended to convey everything was understood: they would all be brothers: they were all becoming Australian mates. Teach them the bushman's bible: teach them the lines of Henry Lawson:

> They call no biped lord or "sir"
> And touch their hat to no man!

Dave also believed the fuzzy-wuzzies had something to teach us — some ancient wisdom from living in such a terrain. They might even help us to lose our guilt about what happened on the Kokoda trail. The fuzzy-wuzzies believed men could expiate their offences. Their men do not have to walk around all their lives like latter-day John Bunyans with burdens on their backs.

"But surely", I replied, "we believe the whole test of being a man consists in being able to bear one's guilt without anaesthetic: that's what our bars are for: and we have our beaches to wash us clean, a dip in the surf at Bondi and a few tinnies to keep up the glow. We despise those who reach for other crutches — God's forgiveness, a hell for oppressors, and Paradise for those who get high marks in the exam of life."

But my friend the poet would have none of this. "What about those", he asked, "who are too fastidious to drown their guilt? What about those who torment themselves for being tormented? If you believe as I do that the only subject that never changes is why men suffer as they do, have you ever thought that the ones who suffered most about the Kokoda trail were the ones who were not even there?"

I asked him if he meant the young Japanese making the long journey from Tokyo, or Osaka, or Yokohama, to the Kokoda trail to find the place where their father died, and stood there in that majestic forest, and spoke to the shade of their father; or young Australians from Sydney or the bush taking the Qantas plane to Port Moresby and hiring a car to drive out to McDonald's Corner from where they could walk to the sites where all the horrors and abominations occurred. I had to go on talking like a historian. So I risked the generalisation that maybe what had happened on the Kokoda trail had saved Port Moresby and other parts of New Guinea from a Sharpeville or a Soweto?

But this idea did not excite him. Historians rarely speak to the human situation. He said he was thinking of those who were the spiritual murderers of the men whose bodies were now rotting in the jungles around Kokoda.

"You mean", I said, "those anti-Fascist gurus who fought for higher civilization in the bars of Melbourne?"

"No", he said, "strangely enough I wasn't thinking of the 'Mitre miserables' or the 'Swanston Family swillers'. Anyhow I think of them with the eye of pity rather than with disdain. I was thinking quite simply of a man who once did evil to another human being. The whole point of the story was that he didn't know what he was doing at the time. It wasn't as though he wanted to hurt anyone, to punish anyone. He looked such a gentle spirit that he wouldn't hurt a fly — and yet there was a devil inside him. Gentle spirits are the greatest monsters of all. The ones who talk about universal brotherhood by day, and lie awake at night plotting how to settle scores with their critics, men with a postgraduate degree in the art of revenge. They are the Davids who have the power to inspire and attract this dumb devotion from the Jonathans of the Australian bush."

"It began with an idyllic moment together. It always does. I suppose that's where it should have ended, but life is uglier than art. The trouble with my story, as with any story, is how much to tell.

The elder of the two was a university student at the time. Study history, he used to say, and you will learn how human beings can change the world. He used to sing Schiller's 'Hymn to Joy', and Henry Lawson's 'We must raise a rebel flag, and sing a rebel chorus'. He was no second-rate European: he was an Australian. The younger fellow's name was Harry, the son of one of the shop-keepers at Cowes on Phillip Island. Charlie and his family used to go there for their annual fishing holiday. I can't tell you much of how it all started, except that Charlie noticed that Harry followed him everywhere, cut the cunje for his bait, put it on his hooks, cleaned his fish. They started to talk about things Charlie said he never spoke to anyone about. Neither wanted to change the other, or improve him. Neither wanted the other to be different from what he was. There were no resentments, no embarrassments.

Harry once asked Charlie whether he believed in God, and Charlie replied that he had a great thirst to believe, but couldn't.

He wanted to believe because he liked to think there was someone who cared what happened to all of us. And Harry asked Charlie whether he believed in life after death. Charlie started to say it all depended on what was meant, how some of the Greeks had believed in the survival of the soul after death, and the difference between Catholic and Protestant teaching on the life after death.

And Harry said: 'Yeah, but what do you think, Charlie?' And again Charlie said he wanted to believe in life after death because he would like to believe we would all see each other again. And Harry took him by the hand, and said it would be good if they saw each other again after they died, and Charlie made a move to take his hand away because . . . but Harry held his hand tighter, and kissed it and cried and Charlie told him he was sure that they would see each other again.

One day at Pyramid Rock Harry asked Charlie to tell him what he thought of Christ. Charlie tried to wriggle out of the answer by saying to Harry: 'Ah, the one without sin — the one who could not overcome death.' And he told Harry that being with Christ plucking the ears of corn in the field must have been like him and Harry climbing up the Nobbies together — those magical moments when he and Charlie felt so towards everyone that he wanted things always to remain as they were. 'That's the meaning, Harry, of those words, "Thy will be done." ' And he did not want to hurt or punish anyone. But what was puzzling was that when Christ went up to Jerusalem, he became very angry, and full of the very loathing he was so free from in those golden days by the lake of Galilee.

On another day when they were fishing off the Red Rock at the Springs west from Pyramid Rock Harry asked Charlie to tell him whether he was a socialist . . . and Charlie told him, yes, he was, because he believed our present society made people angry with each other, and nasty to each other, but that a socialist society would help people to be nicer to each other, and know that tenderness and acceptance Christ had spoken about. Christ was the greatest believer in humanity in the history of mankind because he believed or seemed to believe that men were capable of loving kindness. And Harry said, 'You mean, Charlie, it would be just like the way we feel for each other.' And as they gutted and scaled fish in rock pools, the colour of the star fish, the swaying seaweed, the stripes on the limpets, the periwinkles and the great dome of blue sky, the roar from the sea and the spray like a fine curtain stirred in them a sense of some great mystery, so that a light shone in their eyes when they looked up from the fish and were aware of each other.

It didn't last for long. It never does. In the January of 1936 Harry was not there. His father's business had gone broke, or his mother had shot through — though come to think of it he didn't have a mother, and that might explain why Charlie's talk about the religion of loving kindness moved him so deeply. Anyhow his father became a victim of that monopoly capitalism Charlie had spoken about on the rocks at the Nobbies and Barrie's Beach and Pyramid Rock and Forest's Caves and Smith's Beach. Harry's father was swallowed up, just as the bluenose swallows up the baby sweep, or the black parrot devours the whitebait. Charlie had never explained to Harry why men ever should behave any differently from each other than fish: why the strong wouldn't always prey on the weak. Anyhow Harry became a 'susso' boy in Carlton. His father wandered around the streets of Melbourne with the collar of his coat turned up to make sure that no one could see he was too poor to afford a collar and tie. He still had his pride, and that puzzled hurt look of a man who was asking himself: 'Why did this happen to me?'

Harry drifted into watching the sport on the University Oval; it cost nothing and it was something to do. One day he saw Charlie on the field and waited for him near the gate where the players walked off the field. Harry grabbed him by the hand, and said with all the ardour of the days when they were all in all to each other — 'Charlie' expecting a sign of recognition in return. Harry began to cry and kiss Charlie's hand and asked: 'Don't you remember me, Charlie?'

Charlie slipped his hand away, but made no other gesture, and whispered, 'Give me time to get changed.' Harry dashed off towards Carlton. I don't know whether Charlie was all that much bothered. In those days a hot shower and a few schooners were Melbourne's conscience quieteners. Why should he let them suspect he was possibly a bit of a poofter with a grubby street larrikin? Besides there was bound to be pain when a man cut the cord binding him to his past. A man had to grow up — give up childish things. Besides the rejection of Harry was superseded by offences of a more odious kind. We are all people through whom offences come, and we all live with them as best we can, because unlike the fuzzy-wuzzies we have no ceremony of purification; we are never forgiven; we are never washed clean.

There was a sequel. In 1943 his sister asked Charlie whether he had heard that Harry had been shot dead by a Japanese sniper on the Kokoda tail. When Charlie put on his best mask of indifference she added: 'Poor old Mum and Dad thought you were rather too fond of him: a nice chap but not a brain in his head, not one of our sort.'

And Charlie replied, as he always did to members of his own family, that he had not been specially fond of Harry. This second denial of Harry did not add to his guilt, there was not going to be a third denial, and Charlie was never to hear the cock crow. It was worse than that. By 1944 Charlie had lost his faith. He began to accuse himself of being Harry's murderer. He had filled the heart of an innocent boy, he said, first with a love that he, Charlie, had disowned most wantonly. And he had quite perversely encouraged Harry to fight in the war as a believer when he had lost his own faith."

Well, as a historian I was intrigued to know whether a poet could do justice to all those who were still walking round Australia stained by the guilt of what they did to some of those men who died there. So I said as a historian that we were not likely to find words that would bring comfort to them, because that's the whole trouble with our life, we have no means of expiating our offences. We don't say, "God forgive us all". So we have people like Charlie wandering around the world wearing on their faces an expression of ineffaceable woe. And I believe their suffering is worth a mention in that story of what happened on the Kokoda trail.

A Diet of Bananas and Nietzsche

ONCE upon a time I used to believe quite simply that remark in the book of Jeremiah that the heart is deceitful above all things, and so very wicked that no one can know it. But that was during the days of unleavened bread in Canberra. I had come to think that a remark like that was necessary for me — something between myself and complete despair. Now I had shed such pessimism, shed all the disgust with life, and had begun to talk about all the beauty in the world — about love rather than resignation.

If I had still been hugging that remark about the heart being deceitful above all things like a hot water-bottle to cold, comfortless flesh, I would never have stopped the car to pick up Larry — certainly not in Canberra, where all those organization men were hungry for just a chance to nod and say "I believe Charles Hogan picked up a beardie in Mugga Way."

He looked so unlikely to get the help he was appealing for. He, not just a beardie, but a hair on shoulders man, clothed only in a tattered shirt, and shorts with ragged ends, and shoeless, expect ing one of those glossy, chromiumed diplomatic cars in Mugga Way to give a lift to him. I stopped and asked him where he was going, and when he replied "To Manuka, I guess". The word and the accent telling me straight away at least where he was from, it seemed the least one could do to offer him a cup of tea. He said he did not drink tea, but would be grateful for a glass of water on such a hot day, to which I asked whether he would care for what we in Australia called "something stronger", he replied, "No thanks, I don't drink your Australian beer."

So home he came, where my wife offered him lunch, asking him if he had time for her to mix an omelette. He said he had all the time in the world, but he didn't eat eggs — No, and he didn't eat meat, or fish, or cheese, but yes, he would be grateful for some fruit, some plain brown bread, and a small glass of wine, though the latter was just to be sociable. Then we began to talk about what he was doing in this country.

He told us how he had started a course at a College in New York State, and had gotten a grade A for his English at the end of the first semester. Not one of his teachers spoke about what he was interested in. I asked him was life his subject, he said it was, and that he had decided to leave New York not to be a draft dodger, but to read Nietzsche on the eternal recurrence.

He had hitched lifts to California where he had worked till he had saved a fare to Sydney, from where he had hitched to Cairns to cut cane, and read more Nietzsche. He had spoken to a man who had taught him about food and meditation. He said all this without any sign on the face to show what was going on inside him, though there was a hint or a promise that this restraint had come not so much in the calm after the gusts of passion and wildness had blown through him, but rather as a hint of a man within who had found out something about life. He had perhaps found out the opposite of my own experience of that man within who was never quiet, but was always angry with me, angrier even with me than the world was angry with me, though heaven knows about the dimensions of that anger. His inner quiet did not come from belief, because when I asked him at the appropriate time if he was a believer, he said, "No man, *I don't believe*. Do you?", which made me change the subject, though not before my wife got in her little piece, "That's the question you must never ask him."

The question I had in mind about Larry was not what he believed, but whether he was one of the ones that were bringing everything to ruin — along with the pop singers, flower girls, reefer smokers — I mean one of the many who make me sense the imminence of the cleansing fire at all sorts of odd moments such as a pop singer's frenzy in a TV series, or a hitch-hiker's "see you" after giving him a lift from Canberra to Melbourne, or that panic when you realise that cabinet ministers, vice-chancellors, heads of government departments, judges, footballers, cricketers, musicians, writers and actors do not *know* either.

So I asked Larry whether he wanted to work (wondering whether he, too, was like that insect in Fontaine's fable — which has suddenly become more relevant than Marx on surplus value, or Freud on anal eroticism in the nursery) or so I had come to believe. And Larry said yes, maybe, he could fit in some work before his next period of meditation, and more reading of Nietzsche. As he put it: "I believe that man can help me to become what I am." And when I offered him a few weeks fencing for a few dollars an hour and his keep on the family farm down the south coast where the illustrious Cook saw a "beautiful point" on the coast, he said he would be in it.

Two months later my wife woke me late one night at the coast to tell me Larry had arrived. He was still shoeless with a huge mop of hair like a Restoration rake. I hasten to add I never sniffed decadence or license in Larry, but almost the reverse.

The next morning at breakfast my boy became fascinated with Larry. I remember the only time he looked up from his plate was when Larry said he would only have fruit and water for breakfast. When my wife asked him whether he thought that would give him enough energy to carry corner-posts up a steep hill, Larry said, "I'll be OK" to which my wife added, as though to reassure him that he was one of us despite the voice, the dress and the odd diet, how she agreed that we all ate far too much in Australia.

Then Larry said, "Why don't you all clean yourselves out by going on a monodiet of grapes?"

We all laughed, and I added that in our house we were all on a monodiet of work. My boy chipped in: "Mum and Dad can't think of anything except work."

The fencing went well that day. To the background noise of that great ocean, the thud of surf on sand, the artillery roar of waves crashing over smooth rocks, and the hiss like water on hot metal after the wave has broken, I said to Larry, half serious about the absurdity of what we were doing: "You know, Larry, the aborigines knew nothing about fencing", which caused him to scrutinise my face carefully to see why I indulged in such quaint conceits.

For him the question of ownership of property did not touch the heart of the matter, as my generation had firstly believed, and then ceased to believe, so that all our remarks on life had a flavour of disappointment, just as the early settlers in this country had developed their own sardonic wit to relieve their own disenchantment. But Larry knew nothing about that — and all that had happened since the *Endeavour* first used the Pacific Ocean as its highway touched him not at all.

After lunch, during which Larry quietly swallowed a few dates while the Hogans slipped down grilled drummer, tomato salad, Bega bread and dairy butter, washed down with strong cups of tea, Larry offered to show us some of the exercises he did to prepare himself for meditation. He started with the lotus position, and invited us to try. Our boy managed to get both legs tucked into the correct position, my wife almost managing it. After my repeated failures Larry said that for such cases he recommended a "little Lotus", which I managed to do, but not to sustain. As my boy said: "Gee, Dad, you'd never know you once played cricket."

That night we had visitors. In the two pools of light in the room, two groups had gathered. There was an adult group made up of my wife, complete with knitting, a local dairy farmer, and a woman of indeterminate years who prefaced every remark with the apologia — "You'll get sick of me if I keep talking about myself." My wife said, "My husband never yawns when women talk about their marriages." Which caused our visitor to become weepy for a while, because, as she put it, she had only buried him three months ago that very day, and added: "He couldn't have been nicer — though, mind you, I've only known love once, and that was not in marriage." My wife stopped knitting for the briefest of moments, and I looked over at Larry, who was playing chess with my boy. As ever, there was not a sign on his face that

157

such a remark touched him at all, nor, for that matter, our boy.

My boy broke the silence by asking Larry how he started, to which he replied, "By going on a fast for three days".

After the guests had gone, I asked Larry why he wore the uniform of a drop-out, hoping the word "uniform" might needle him into uncovering what was going on inside him.

"I wouldn't call it a uniform."

"What I'm trying to say is whether this is your way of protesting against what your parents wanted you to do."

"My parents didn't urge me to wear the clothes of the Kennedy clean-cuts back home."

"No, I meant you thought they wanted you to be a clean-cut. So you expressed yourself by having long hair rather than the short-cropped, Julius Caesar fringe of the State Department models."

"I don't know about that. Sounds kind of academic to me."

"Well, let me put it this way. Do you think the clothes you wear, and all that you do, are one way of ensuring that you remain in the playground of childhood for a hell-of-a-long time . . . that they are just another sign of you never having learned discipline . . . of never having been made afraid . . . of long hair as the fruits of permissiveness in the nursery, the home and the classroom."

"Maybe . . . but you see, I loved my father . . . No, really, I loved him."

There was silence for a moment, broken only by the uproar from the sea, which was not unlike the uproar inside all of us, always there, but sometimes more turbulent than at others. At the risk of seeming to needle him, when all I wanted to do was to find out what he lived by, I went on with the idea, or rather a connection that had come to me during the silence —

"Do you see any connection, Larry, between a diet of bananas and reading Nietzsche?"

"No"

"Well, I do."

"Fire away."

So I did.

"Do you think this diet of bananas is your way of saying you have retained the innocence of childhood . . . it's your lasting playground symbol . . . while Nietzsche satisfies all those aggressions, that will to dominate which a permissive childhood never eradicated. So that now you make your gestures of peace, the Hindu clasp of the hands, sitting in the Lotus position, meditating on the eight-fold path to non-attachment, while secretly enjoying Nietzsche's remark — what is it? — if you must go to the women, make sure you take a good whip. I'm never sure of the exact words of any quotation, am notoriously unreliable, but that is the spirit of his work . . . a constant titillation of our sensual cruelty by the world's greatest timidity pervert, a guaranteed emotional bath, or what I would call a do-it-your-own kit for the timid."

Once again he made no reply. My wife used to say there was nothing to touch the arrogance of the drop-out men. They despised us all as money-grubbers, conformists and grovellers before the god of success, and believed we had even forfeited the right to be spoken to. They looked to the children to carry on their work. I had wanted to ask Larry whether he was interested in Christ's remark — "Unless ye become as little children . . . ".

Before I could do this I noticed there was one person who hung on every word Larry uttered. That was my boy. The next morning he announced at breakfast that he would only be drinking water that day, as Larry had persuaded him to go on a diet of bananas after a fast of three days to clean himself out. I began to tell him to be his age. No one could fish from the rocks on an empty stomach. But my wife winked at me. When the boy followed Larry out to the verandah for the daily pre-meditation exercises, she told me to let hunger rather than parental anger bring the boy to his senses.

At lunch there was no change. Larry and the boy contented themselves with a tumbler of water while we made our way through boiled fish, tomato salad, bread and cheese and jasmine tea. All of this was taken in silence, as even our boy felt called upon to break that silence by saying through a nervous giggle, "Dad's beginning to frown." To which Larry commented, "It looks as though I am not the only one here who takes Nietzsche for his spiritual food. Seems like your father takes him in pretty big gulps."

This did not improve the atmosphere as we prepared for the afternoon visit to the rocks. By lunch-time the nor'easter had freshened enough to stir up white horses on the waves far out to sea, and to leave a carpet of white foam inshore. As we put the tomahawk and long knife in the bucket for the cunje, and oiled the ferrules on the rods, and tested the reels, I told my boy it was just the sort of sea which lures the big drummer to strike at the cunje . . . "They love it, boy." But on this day he seemed to lack the energy to respond to my mood, or perhaps Larry had been putting ideas into his head about fishermen being murderers.

As we made our way through the bush towards the cliff-top my own excitement caused me to risk yet another probe into Larry's mind. Just as we pushed in between two Grevillea bushes, covered in flower, I asked him how he liked the Australian bush. He said, "I guess I find it kind of dry."

By the time we had clambered over the rocks to the point where we wanted to fish, the wind had strengthened. The waves were spraying the spot where we normally cut cunje, not strong enough to knock a man over, but enough to wet him through. I tried one of my father's old tricks — one, he said, he had learned from his own father — "Do you think, boy, you're strong enough to cut cunje there or do you want me to do it today?" He took the tomahawk out of the bucket, and sprang down on the shelf on which cunje, sea anemones, mussels, limpets and cochineal shells were growing in wild profusion — as well as the rock lettuce. I had vowed never to warn the boy how slippery and treacherous it was, knowing he would only say mockingly, "Here beginneth my father's first lesson on treachery — both vegetable and human." Like my wife he knew all too well what was inside me.

But today I could not forebear, because with each step he slipped and stumbled till I said "God spare my days, have I sired a man who can't stand up?" But, thank God, before I began to joke at his expense, I sensed it was physical weakness, not some innate clumsiness, that was causing him to slip.

He hacked away at the cunje. Like his foot his eye faltered. He missed the soft spot for the blade just where the shell adhered to the rock face. I was wondering whether to joke again: to remind him that "With C and G's you see with ease." He was far too young to know "C and G" made spectacles.

A huge wave broke on the shelf in front of him, and sprayed over all of us, and I heard his shout of terror above the great roar of the sea, and saw his legs cut away from under him as the water was sucked back again into the sea. I jumped down into the shelf and grabbed him by the right wrist just as his body began to slide down the face of that slippery shelf into the sea, and was about to say to him, "For God's sake never come near an angry ocean again on an empty stomach", when I saw that Larry had also taken hold of his left wrist, and was looking at me as though he wanted to say something quite different, and did in fact say over the roar of the sea something that I made out to be, "Why feel pity and terror in the face of something from everlasting?"

But by then I had decided that words would not be adequate with Larry. From that day I only spoke to Larry about trivial things — and certainly never again about a diet of bananas and Nietzsche.

Also published by Penguin

MEMORIES OF THE ASSASSINATION ATTEMPT AND OTHER STORIES

Gerard Windsor

A man spars with his wife over his dead mother-in-law's unopened wedding presents; a deserted woman is visited by the father of her child; an old priest relives a tragedy in which his own youthful idealism was instrumental; an urbane gynaecologist discovers there are some parts of his women that retaliate . . .

The reach and range of Gerard Windsor's imagination has already been critically acclaimed: 'fabulist, moralist and humorist all at once'. His stories reflect experiences that span the sensual to the spiritual, the mundane to the macabre, yet beneath all their irony lurk subtle compassion and moral concern. This fine new collection can only assure his reputation as one of Australia's most deft and engaging fiction writers.

Of his first short-story collection, *The Harlots Enter First,* critics said: '. . . remarkable talent' (Elizabeth Riddell, *Bulletin*); 'a startling imagination . . . a craftsman in the best sense' (Mary Lord, *Australian Book Review)*

STORIES OF THE WATERFRONT

John Morrison

'John was born in England, but no native-born reflects the spirit of Australia more than he does. This country, of which he is so much a part, has absorbed and recreated him as one of its most significant voices.'

Alan Marshall

These imaginative and sensitive stories begin at a time when wharfies turned up at the docks to be picked like cattle, and often went home without work or pay. The events range from personal dilemmas like sharing lottery winnings to coping with pig-headed bosses and the tragedy of sudden death.

John Morrison worked for ten years on the Melbourne waterfront in the 1930s and '40s. His *Stories of the Waterfront,* collected here for the first time, give a realistic yet unusually sympathetic account of the much-maligned wharfie.

Set in the years after the turbulent times depicted in the television film, *Waterfront,* the book provides a narrative of improvement of conditions and the constant struggle to maintain them by a group of warm and down-to-earth people.

A WINDOW IN MRS X's PLACE
Selected Short Stories

Peter Cowan

Peter Cowan has been compared to writers as diverse as Hemingway and Lawson as he 'explores the responses of individuals to crises in love and work against a variety of Australian, especially Western Australian, land, sea and city scapes.'

This selection by Bruce Bennett allows his work to be 'experienced as a continuity, ranging from stories published in a variety of magazines and collections since the early 1940s. During that period, Cowan has established a well deserved reputation as master craftsman in one of the most difficult art forms.'

'One of the finest two or three short story writers now working in Australia.' T.A.G. Hungerford, Weekend News, *1965*.

'To the negative side of life he is as spring to the bare winter tree.' Thelma Forshaw, Sydney Morning Herald *1973*

'Cowan has continued to experiment with the short story form, to test its flexibility, its possibilities.' Bruce Williams, The Literature of Western Australia *1980*.

THE STATE OF THE ART
The Mood of Contemporary
Australia in Short Stories

Introduced and edited by Frank Moorhouse

A frenetic, talented guitarist, barely hanging on to a fragmented life; a canny Jewish uncle, frustrated without a family to organise; lovers seeking pleasure. Whatever the cost; an old woman, trundled from the home of one son to another, an intrusion, unloved . . .

These are among the characters, some innocent, some eccentric, some disillusioned, who are portrayed in this striking, innovative collection of short stories. Their diversity of style and content reflects the robust hedonism of contemporary Australian society.